ASTRAL DEBRIS
A Quiddity in Prose and Poetry

D. Sidney-Fryer has written or edited the following books:

Poems in Prose, by Clark Ashton Smith (1965)
Etchings in Ivory, poems in prose by Robert E. Howard (1968)
Other Dimensions, short stories by Clark Ashton Smith (1970)
Songs and Sonnets Atlantean: The First Series (1971)
Selected Poems, omnibus by Clark Ashton Smith (1971)
The Last of the Great Romantic Poets, i.e., Clark Ashton Smith (1973)
Emperor of Dreams: A Clark Ashton Smith Bibliography (1978)
The Black Book of Clark Ashton Smith, his commonplace book (1979)
A Vision of Doom, poems by Ambrose Bierce (1980)
The City of the Singing Flame, tales by Clark Ashton Smith (1981)
The Last Incantation, tales by Clark Ashton Smith (1982)
The Monster of the Prophecy, tales by Clark Ashton Smith (1983)
Strange Shadows: The Uncollected Fiction and Essays of Clark Ashton Smith, edited
    by Steve Behrends with Donald Sidney-Fryer and Rah Hoffman (1989)
The Hashish-Eater; or, The Apocalypse of Evil, 1922 version, by Clark Ashton
    Smith (1990; with CD 2008 performed by D. Sidney-Fryer)
As Green as Emeraude: The Collected Poems of Margo Skinner (1990)
The Devil's Notebook (complete epigrams and apothegms) by Clark Ashton
    Smith, edited with Don Herron (1990)
Songs and Sonnets Atlantean: The Second Series (2003)
Gaspard de la Nuit, by Aloysius Bertrand, translation (2004)
Songs and Sonnets Atlantean: The Third Series (2005)
The Atlantis Fragments: The "Songs and Sonnets Atlantean," omnibus
    (2008, 2009)
The Outer Gate: The Collected Poems of Nora May French (2009)
The Golden State Phastasticks: The California Romantics and Related Subjects:
    Collected Essays and Reviews, edited with Leo Grin and Alan Gullette
    (2011)
The Atlantis Fragments, The Novel: The Existing Chronicle: A Vision of the
    Final Days (2011)
Hobgoblin Apollo: The Autobiography of Donald Sidney-Fryer (2016)
Odds & Ends (poetry, 2016)
West of Wherevermore and Other Travel Writings (2016)
Aesthetics Ho! Essays on Art, Literature, and Theatre (2017)
Ends and Odds (poetry, 2017)
The Case of the Light Fantastic Toe: The Romantic Ballet and Signor Maestro
    Cesare Pugni—A Chronicle and Source Book (magnum opus, 2018)
West of Wherevermore and Other Essays (second version, 2019) /
    The Miscellaneon (poetry, 2019)
A King Called Arthor and Other Morceaux (2020)
Random Notes, Random Lines (2021)
Astral Debris: A Quiddity in Prose and Poetry (2023)

Astral Debris

A QUIDDITY IN PROSE AND POETRY

D. Sidney-Fryer

Hippocampus Press

New York

Published by Hippocampus Press
P.O. Box 641, New York, NY 10156
www.hippocampuspress.com

Cover artwork by Daniel V. Sauer, dansauerdesign.com.
Hippocampus Press logo designed by Anastasia Damianakos.

First Edition
1 3 5 7 9 8 6 4 2
ISBN 978-1-61498-399-6

Contents

STAR DREK

A new series

––––––––

Garbage Scows in Outer Space
—a quiddity in prose—

I. A New Discovery

Please dot your i's and cross your t's,
But don't forget your A B C'S,
And thank you, nor your X Y Z's.
                                        Old Rime.

From the bridge of the supercargo space ship, the transfer giant 5421, to the Space Control Center Alphabet in permanent orbit between planet Earth and planet Moon.

"Navigator Chris Owens here, now circling over Transfer Planet DYT 989. Over."

"Nate Hilger here at Alphabet. Tell the captain to proceed to unload whenever conditions allow an easy transit down to the surface, to transfer the accumulated cargo onto the next available terrain. How does it look?"

Chris: "The same as usual. Why do you ask?"

Nate: "Do you remember that environmental news item that I sent you some little time back? In case you don't, I'll send it along with a recent, rather negative, update from the *New York Times*. Let me summarize it for you now. You might want to record what I have to say, so set it up now and I'll wait. [Pause.] Okay? Okay. Here I go.

"As you know (you hail from the Big Apple), New York City has been dumping—its trash, its garbage, organic or inorganic—for years and years (maybe centuries by now) east or southeast of New York harbor. Most of the stuff, the heavy trash, falls down onto the ocean floor, more or less onto the same general place. The local fish also consume some of it.

"Well, the authorities found some new species living down there, half ichthyoid, half water-breathing humanoid. Wisely the authorities did not permit any films of this to be released to the media. Films or videos would only have made the whole issue even worse and more complicated than what it became.

"This was and is rather startling news all over our solar system and our galaxy. Even some of the further galaxies could not help but respond. At first the authorities wanted the deep-sea divers to destroy these new species. But such an outcry arose and came from all the inhabited planets throughout our galaxy that they, the harassed authorities, decided to let things happen as they would without human interference.

"Yes, let me emphasize that! They would let things happen as they would, existentially. Now it appears that there are more than a few novel species living down there on the ocean bottom. The United Nations has now stepped in, to speak for and to protect them as legitimate living creatures. The local and federal governments are cooperating, bless them all.

"What the bigwigs at the space station here, not to mention the V.I.P.s in Washington, in our dear U.S. government, want your captain to do—once you finish dumping, oops, transferring, the accumulated cargo down onto the ground—is to reconnoitre the oldest heaps or mounds of trash, maybe even to send down a special crew, to find out if something similar may not yet have occurred in certain localities, above all the older multi-level accumulations. Over."

Chris: "It sounds like a big job. This planet has now accumulated so much trash and animal refuse, including human stuff, that it has already created its own methane atmosphere. We'll see what we'll find. I'll pass all this on, first to our commander. Captain Verne Laverne has been following those developments southeast of New York City with fervid interest. Like me, he's from the Big Apple. Thanks for the update. Have no fear, I shall get back to you anon. Over."

Chris had recorded what Nate had told him over the Internet, and soon he would release it to the captain. With Verne Laverne he had formed a real friendship apart from the obligatory give-and-take in military terms between captain and navigator. Earlier in life they had both become chess enthusiasts, even studying the earliest history of the game in Hindustan, otherwise Mother India.

As an aside Chris ruefully considered how the Super Drive aboard rocket ships, or spacecraft, had enabled so much further discovery and exploration among the further stars (but not overly far distant—limits existed still), but now the M.S.D., or Maximum Super Drive, had extended the range of possibilities even further, needing only superior spacecraft (veritable ocean liners as it were) to take advantage of the M.S.D., plus first and foremost the essential, if not the quintessential, financing from a given government or a consortium of zillionaire investors.

As a further aside Chris further considered, also ruefully, certain ingredients among the purely human or humanoid components: the results of abortions natural or surgically induced, the sanitary napkins employed and then thrown away by mostly human females, not to mention the organic materials from human hospitals and veterinary ones.

He pondered even further the organic refuse of non-human activity (farm animals and the rest, beef cattle, dairy cattle, pigs, goats, sheep, horses and similar quadrupeds), defecation and urination of every type whether human or non-human, and all this mixed in with lawn and landscape leavings and cuttings of every description and variety, not to mention all manner of organic material clandestinely introduced by sundry humans or humanoids. What alchemy or chemistry would not result from all that mixture? An outcome fascinating to contemplate!

Chris cogitated for awhile to himself, while he thought about the implications of what Nate had informed him, no less than its implications for Transfer Planet DYT 989. Then a novel and awesome idea struck him like a bolt of lightning, with all the possibilities of yet further future implications. Humankind had merrily gone on its way somewhat heedless of the consequences of its actions. What had not developed then on all the transfer planets in other solar systems and in other galaxies? Awesome prospect indeed, if not in fact, then in palpable reality!

The authorities had chosen the planets utilized in this mode, as dumps or transfer points in this (ahem) experiment, because they seemed lifeless and without atmosphere. Now the humans on or from planet Earth had inadvertently once again created without intending to do so an (ahem) interesting physical and moral problem wherever they had transferred their innocent garbage, or so they thought, or had not thought. What hath Human Being not wrought?

Chris had downloaded into print form (the captain was old-fashioned and liked the printed page over most other media) what Nate had recorded for him. Chris would now drop it off on the captain's desk. The navigator expected consequences like those following a significant move in chess. Indeed, what hath human or humanoid not wrought?

At 7:00 P.M. the captain buzzed Chris on the space ship's intercom. He answered at once: "Yes, Captain!"

The captain: "Could you come to my cabin at 7:30? I want to discuss this report from our good friend Nate at Alphabet. I've ordered supper for both of us, and some drinks. We'll need them."

At 7:30 the captain opened his cabin door and escorted Chris into the main chamber of the captain's own suite. Here the captain conducted much of the ship's direction and business. They embraced with an extra warmth. Although neither happened to be gay, they remained very close and relied much on each other. The friendship was better than a love affair, because it did not depend on or include a sexual relationship.

They sat them down at the oval table in the main or front chamber. Soon a steward entered with a large tray containing drinks and food. After a preliminary chat, they ate in silence. When they finished, they sat back each with their several drinks, fairly strong as neither used much mixer.

The captain, handsome and athletic like Chris, and just a little older, smiled and then winked at his close friend. "Chris, I need to consult with you, as I can with nobody else."

Chris: "Fire away," grinning and winking back at Verne, always on a first-name basis when no one else was around.

Verne: "So what do you think?"

Chris: "Not an easy or pleasant mission."

Verne: "As the captain I'm expected to lead not just the investigation but also the investigative squadron, which I can do. I'd rather just send the squadron down. Would you like to join us?"

Chris: "Perhaps not on the first expedition, but maybe on the second. But first let's dump our very full cargo on the new designated terrain, have the hull cleaned, and then reconnoitre some of the older multi-level accumulations. But first let's do as much as we can with the special sensors on the ship."

Verne: "We think the same. You would make a good captain. Let's sleep on it. Meanwhile, before we both retire, what say that we watch an old and very charming Hollywood movie of the mid-1930s?"

Chris: "Which one is that?"

Verne: "*It Happened One Night.* What say?"

Chris: "I love that film. It always puts me in a pleasant and, yes, nostalgic mood. Neither of us needs an epic film given our present circumstances!"

As he fell asleep in his own cabin (after the movie in the captain's quarters), Chris reflected with relief that the captain had assistants who worked, as they did, in regular shifts. The navigator also reflected with the same sense of relief on how the regular workday, the twenty-four-hour day, even aboard a space ship or at a space station (just as it did back on Earth), fell into the three main shifts per custom and human comfort: 12 A.M. to 8 A.M.—

8 A.M. to 4 P.M.—4 P.M. to 12 A.M. After teasing these periods of time in his head, Chris fell sound asleep and slept a full eight hours. He did not need to report for duty at the usual navigational console in the navigator's control room. He had the day off.

The captain had already chosen the special crew that he would lead down onto the surface of Transfer Planet DYT 989. That is, as soon as the giant transfer ship 5421 could finish transferring its huge malodorous cargo down onto the planetary surface. That would require several days. Then the hull, the gigantic interior of the space craft, would undergo the usual major cleaning. The latter always took several days.

Verne had invited Chris to his cabin (or suite) for another discussion before the captain would lead his special crew down onto ground zero, or not so zero.

Verne: "You'll remember our discussion of the other day. We made a perfunctory enumeration of the trash, the garbage, that the ordinary transfer ship accumulates and carries until it is deposited on some transfer planet." Chris nodded at what the captain said.

Verne: "The long-term use of the designation *organic* has led most people mostly to associate it with plants—produce, such as fruits and vegetables. But of course it also involves animal and human physical particulars. The leavings of hospitals and hospices, the aftermath of many human activities, never mind of slaughterhouses from the preparation of meat for human consumption. Overall quite a complicated mixture, no? The big question is: what might not have occurred in these miasmal deposits? Yes, we are both thinking of the same thing: the body parts and bodily leavings from humans and animals, the non-humans."

Verne paused, and smiled: "Chris, are you sure that you are not eager to join us in our first official reconnaissance?" He asked this with a certain ironic slyness.

Chris: "I'll go down with you and the special crew during the second expedition, as I've already decided. Meanwhile, I pray that these new body suits, this new armor as it were, will not fail you and your special detachment." Chris did not smile at this point.

Verne: "We are on the same page, in sync with each other. You did not sleep so well last night, and neither did I!"

Chris: "Inadvertently, the body and the psyche seem to have their own programs and prerogatives—that is, separate! You and I seem to be operating in a strong post-adolescent condition. We're both as horny as teenagers. Eventually (I hope) we'll both settle down and sleep much better than just tossing and turning, and only half-sleeping."

Verne: "Amen to that! We'll talk later, and of course after this first expedition scheduled early tomorrow morning."

After the immense cargo ship had landed, or almost landed, hovering above the ground, it disgorged its accumulated contents. Then after its thorough cleansing (this had involved much of the crew), the transfer giant 5421 went back into orbit around Transfer Planet DYT 989. The overall procedure had required about a week; it always varied a little in time, sometimes more, sometimes less. Everyone wore body armor for the cleansing.

At last came the morning scheduled for the captain to lead

the special group of six trained astronauts. Everyone had put on the new body suits, the "new armor" as dubbed by Chris. They were using one of the space dories, the vastly smaller spacecraft that they kept aboard ship for easy access between a planet and the gigantic mother vessel usually in orbit around the latter.

The captain had selected one of the oldest, multi-level, or multi-deposit areas that the transfer ships had established almost at the start of the initial dumping on this especial planet. The captain had planned their first investigation for no more than three or four hours; that is, as it might result, barring accidents or unforeseen complications due to the uncertain terrain and its chemical composition. Unless an emergency happened, the captain and his special group would pursue their mission without undue communication.

As it was, they stayed in that particular area beneath investigation for a full four hours, even if the oxygen devices that each carried in his body suit could have given them at least a few more. The space dory carried them back to the mother ship, safe and sound. After they doffed their new body armor, they returned to their individual cabins. Meanwhile several crew members, also wearing protective clothing, thoroughly cleansed the new-style space suits, ready for use on another day.

Later during the latter afternoon the six astronauts convened in the captain's own suite: to effect an initial survey, to discuss what they had seen, to compare notes, and to do an initial survey of what their hand-held cameras had recorded on film. No one said anything to the other crew members on Transfer Ship 5421. Until the captain gave out the news aboard the vessel, the astronauts remained silent, as custom and protocol had long since established themselves.

The captain spoke over the ship's intercom. "Greetings to the personnel aboard Transfer Ship 5421. Our initial investigation on Transfer Planet DYT 989 has gone well. We shall make a more abundant report later, probably tomorrow. We discovered much of interest. We plan our second and last expedition for the day after tomorrow. Thank you for your help and attention." The captain remained a stickler for ordinary politeness, but not always in military terms.

He then invited the navigator via the intercom to his cabin for a rendezvous at 7:30 P.M., again including drinks and a meal. As ever, Verne escorted Chris to the oval conference table that also served for eating.

Verne: "I ordered us each a couple of extra drinks. Even if you may not need them, I do. Yes, after today's expedition!"

Chris: "So you found much of interest? I gather from your tone that it did not seem especially pleasant."

At this moment the steward entered with the tray of drinks and the two plates of edibles. Verne had him place the tray on the table between captain and navigator in their status as officers.

As he hoisted his first cocktail up to his lips, Verne smiled ruefully and said, "That is an understatement!" After an initial swallow he sighed, "That tastes great!" He continued to drink, and then he spoke again.

"We are no strangers to the appearance of these transfer planets, especially the older ones, and their older parts with stuff very well accumulated. But we usually see the garbage from orbit or from just above the ground when the ship hovers to discharge the huge cargo garnered from selected sites on many planets. However, to get down on the surface and investigate up close the oldest accumulations is quite a different story. I really don't want to go down again on the second expedition the day after tomorrow, but I have no choice. Headquarters has mandated at least a second one, or more if we as the investigators feel that it is needed."

Verne had lowered his gaze to his plate, then looked directly again at Chris, who said, "I can well imagine what you saw, that is, up close."

The captain continued: "In our official reports we speak of the oldest accumulations as multi-level, almost as if we spoke of multi-level buildings. The more recent deposits don't remain at one level, but merge and become somewhat mixed in with the older and, er, riper ones. The overall result is a god-awful mess made up of everything that we consider extremely repulsive. In our everyday lives on a planet we can flush the toilet or throw something in the garbage container, if we don't get rid of it down the sink via the so-called garbage disposal. A rather generic name, no?"

Chris nodded back at Verne and said quietly, "Indeed!"

Verne: "I'm greatly relieved that we could not smell the stuff where we were investigating, or anywhere on the planet where we have already dumped. Whether this squares with orthodox science or not, there seems to be an emanation, an effluvium, right above the oldest deposits . . . maybe the start of an atmosphere. And yes, there is at least one new species of life. It doesn't seem to need oxygen, but only the gas generated within the garbage deposits. We saw a few colonies here and there. The creatures look like giant larvae, but we saw no chrysalises from which some kind of adult could emerge."

Chris continued nursing his drink as Verne spoke again. "Incidentally, if you decide not to accompany us on our second and (I hope) last expedition, you have that option."

Chris: "No, I still want to go down with you. I still want to see the older deposits up close. Let's eat and watch some old movie."

The next day the captain over the ship's intercom reported in greater detail, mentioning the colonies of what looked like giant larvae. Perhaps, he added, he could give more information after the second expedition scheduled for tomorrow.

Came the new day when the captain, the six astronauts, and the navigator had all made themselves ready for the second investigation by 7:00 A.M. In his own turn Chris found the new space suits comfortable and lightweight to wear while walking and manoeuvering . . . the new improved oxygen device functioned with no problem.

The group took one of the space dories down to another older accumulation but next to the one explored the day before yesterday. Everything went smoothly. Chris had his wish to see the oldest garbage up close. As the captain had averred, it had all resulted in a god-awful mess, a mix of everything that humans might find extremely repulsive whether organic or inorganic. Yes, Chris like the captain felt relieved that he could not smell these older deposits.

Metaphorically he could only liken it to a kaleidoscopic mixture of Hieronymus Bosch, the Breughels, and Salvador Dalí, but without the philtre of their craftsmanship and artistry; and also mixed in with the leavings of death camps or slaughterhouses.

The captain and his group did not linger. They had seen little that was new to them. Just as they were going back to the space dory, Chris received a major shock. As he was turning from a high ledge of god-awful stuff, he noticed a hole at eye level, the entrance to a very small tunnel. Out of it, but not attacking him, a small creature rather like a furry rodent poked his head, looking directly at the navigator.

Chris at once noticed the intensity and intelligence of the creature's violet-eyed gaze. Then the rodent, or whatever it was, disappeared back inside the tunnel, probably returning to his lair. *It was an entity plumb out of a nightmare.*

The navigator bottled up his reaction, one of great fright and confusion; he said nothing to the others via the intercom that operated among their space suits. Silently he joined the others in the space dory that then returned to the mother ship. Chris at first decided to say nothing about his close encounter with the alien creature. All of a sudden he longed to go back (what a desperate feeling!) to a regular planet like Earth, if not that home ambiance itself. The time had come at any rate for Transfer Ship 5421 to return home so that the crew could have a regular and major vacation as mandated by law, following a prolonged voyage in outer space.

Chris decided that, if he did tell the captain about his encounter, it would happen off the record, and as something between them strictly as friends. He would first request his silence, to keep the alien encounter to himself or to their discussion of it. They could confer during their usual evening meal together. Meanwhile for the rest of the day the captain and the head navigator attended to the multifarious responsibilities of their respective occupations.

After their evening meal, Verne looked inquiringly at Chris, and asked, "Well, what did you think?"

Chris: "Yes, a god-awful mess and mixture, and yes, I was relieved like you that I could not exercise my sense of smell. I doubt that I'll ever *wish* to see an old garbage deposit up close again. But thanks for the opportunity!"

All at once they burst out laughing heartily, relieving the tension that the disgusting environment on the planet below them had inspired.

Chris: "I did have an interesting experience, er, encounter, but first I enjoin your silence. Let's keep it to ourselves. You need not include it in your official report. Okay? This is only between us as friends."

Verne: "Why, Chris, of course, if you put it that way. I'll shut everything off that might accidentally record our consultation."

Chris: "Thanks!" And then he related the alien encounter. "I was so disoriented by the fright and confusion that assailed me that I did what I usually do in such a situation, when I feel physically threatened, unless it involves the safety of others. I bottle up while I prepare to fight. In this case there was no one else, and no harm done.

"I would rather not make an official report of it, and I ask you as my friend to keep it between us. Okay?"

Verne: "It's okay. When I make my report back to Space Control Center Alphabet, I'll only mention what I and the others found or did not find. Let me put everything back on that might have recorded us. Changing the subject, what about another old movie, a real dandy, an early sci-fi classic, *2001: A Space Odyssey?*"

Chris: "Agreed! One of my favorite films of all time, up there with *Gone with the Wind!*"

The next day at noon Verne called Chris to his cabin and spoke. "I just made my official report back to space headquarters. I mentioned only what the others of us found in the course of the two expeditions. Only we know concerning your alien encounter. All is well, but thanks for your honesty with me as your friend.

"Headquarters commanded me to return the ship back to Mother Earth. If they want to pursue the matter of the giant larvae, or whatever, they can have the next gigantic transfer ship handle it on their own for headquarters. So we can now head home."

Chris: "Perfect! Not quite happily ever after, but the next best thing to it. That was a close encounter that just avoided possible disaster or injury, not to mention messy consequences. Yes, let's go home!"

Verne and Chris happily smiled at each other.

II. A Big Decision

The supercargo spacecraft, the transfer giant 5421, had almost reached its home base, the Big Home Harbor, in and around the Space Control Center Alphabet. There both the harbor and the center floated in permanent orbit between planet Earth and the moon. The latter had long since acquired its own chief colony or city, as self-contained and self-supporting as possible, with vast greenhouse farms. The moon lay thus beyond the further metaphorical shores of the Big Home Harbor. That general ambiance, a prime locale, served as the point where the smaller service and supply ships came from Earth.

They came to re-supply the bigger ships, particularly the big cruise liners, but first to remove special cargo (not garbage nor trash) as well as to transport any passengers or crew from any long-term or short-term voyages. The extended voyages represented the longest ones, usually no more than four-year assignments. From this locale the biggest ships would embark back out into the real outer space, whether the luxurious cruise liners, gigantic in their own way and special in their much shorter voyages, or the giant specialist ships usually gone for four years on special missions involving discovery and exploration amid the closer galaxies.

As expected, the United States supervised the Big Home Harbor and managed the space control hub. However, other countries helped in the administration of these focal points but strictly under the supervision of the United Nations. The crews whose spacecraft were coming back from the longest voyages found themselves in a state of eager anticipation to return to the home planet, as well as to their families and close friends.

Shortly before arriving at the Big Home Harbor, Chris had a discussion with Verne in the privacy of the captain's own suite. The captain instructed his secretary not to disturb them except in an emergency.

Chris: "I don't know just how you feel about it, right at this exact moment, but not only am I eager beaver about sojourning on dear old Mother Earth for awhile, but I'm more than eager to spend some significant stretches of time with dear Jeanie, if she will still have me back among her current line-up of lovers. People can certainly change during four long years. While the ladies and gentlemen in our government-supervised brothels aboard ship can surely take care of most of us while on a long voyage—and *we* all have our favorites—there is nothing like enjoying one's own particular lover!"

Verne: "I heartily concur. I'm sure my earthbound wife and I, not to mention our kids, are all eager for us to meet up again. After our extensive gardens aboard ship, where we grow our own fresh fruit and vegetables, and after the artificial pastures where we grow the animals for our fresh meat, I'm almost as eager to see the fresh fields and pastures that make our home planet the delectable paradise that it remains!"

Chris: "Agreed! Even if the gardens and pastures aboard ship concern you as the captain far more and not me as the humble chief navigator. But I'm having a midlife crisis. Let me explain, as I've been keeping it to myself."

Verne: "Fire away!"

Chris: "Verne, I have now completed, as have you, four

long, four-year missions with long vacations in between. But these extended voyages are eating away at me. We are very well paid, that's true. I'm debating whether I should continue with the transfer giants or switch on over to the big cruise liners for a healthy change.

"The liners make cruises that rarely exceed a year or half a year. The pay is almost as good as what we get on the big transfer ships. The Outer Space Consortium amply rewards us, yes. But still . . ."

Verne: "I hear what you say, and I follow you. Continue."

Chris: "The cruise liners are super-luxurious, very comfortable, and they cater to a special and very wealthy clientele. For captain and crew the ships represent a choice assignment indeed. It would be great if you might also want a change for awhile. You could switch on over with me. Maybe we could arrange it with the bigwigs in the consortium. Ditto with the V.I.P.s down there in Washington, D.C. What do you think?"

Verne looked very thoughtful. "Maybe you're right. Maybe I need a big change myself. Let me think it over. We have talked about it before, at the start of this last voyage."

Chris looked as thoughtful as Verne. "Yes, we have, but I am in dead earnest about it this time. No ands, ifs, or buts."

Verne walked over to the big window bay, followed by Chris. From the wide window—a big picture one, almost as large as one in a department store—they had an unmatched view of the nocturnal planet, Mother Earth, the side now presented to those aboard ship. No competition from the moon: its dark side was behind them.

The captain spoke, almost with tears in his eyes. "There she is, our mother, our original home. How beautiful she looks after dark with all the manmade lights!"

"Yes," Chris quietly concurred, but he spoke further. "I want to see more of our home planet. A radical change from a gigantic transfer ship to a giant cruise liner would surely guarantee our seeing more of Earth than what we are doing now. Okay?" He looked fixedly into his companion's eyes.

Verne: "Okay! Once we return to Earth, let's apply together for the big change to a different kind of space vessel. But let's do so as soon as possible. And don't forget: there's a lot of competition for such choice assignments. However, our own past performance aboard various spacecrafts will certainly speak in our favor. And maybe both of us can pull a few strings here and there!"

Chris: "We are agreed, the first big step. Let's sleep on it tonight before we return to Mother Earth in the morning."

Verne grinned back and simply said, "Agreed!"

The next morning captain and navigator met in the lobby, the main entrance and departure area before descending aboard the special smaller spacecraft that would return them and many others back to their true home base.

They had both dressed in one of their fanciest officer uniforms. They looked handsome and official in their natty attire. They had sent their luggage ahead of them aboard the special smaller spacecraft.

Verne smiled at Chris: "Well, how do you feel about your big decision today?"

Chris grinned back at him: "All the stronger! And you?"

Verne: "I could not feel more certain!"

Chris: "After we have each settled in at home, let's get in touch, say, in a few days. Then we'll go from there, all right?"

Verne nodded back, whispering playfully, "Aye-aye, Captain!" They embraced and got ready to go to the departure station, to take the designated spacecraft that would transport them back at last to their dear home planet.

They were "Going ashore!"

III. Navigating Ashore

Several days passed, if not a week, before captain and navigator got back in touch with each other. Chris phoned Verne first. "Hi, how's it going?"

Verne: "Okay overall, but some big changes happened while I've been gone. The kids have all flown the coop. They are still in college or grad school, or they have moved out to live on their own. I've told my wife—Antaea, as you may recall—about us wanting to change from our interstellar garbage scows to cruise liners with their much shorter voyages. She also really wants me to do so. She said that, if I did not, she would divorce me. I did give her carte blanche long ago to take up with any apt lover when I'm absent."

Chris: "Well now, you have even greater incentive to go with me to the big home office north of Manhattan. Convenient for us that we don't have to go far to get there. As for my lover, Jeanie got tired of waiting for me, got herself married, and now has a kid with Sean, her husband. A big surprise! But Sean is being kind and generous. He's allowing Jeanie and me to spend a little private time together at my place . . . for old times' sake."

Verne: "Wow, some decent guy! I'd like to meet him. Meanwhile I'll arrange an appointment for us next week up the Hudson at headquarters. As soon as I have the date and day, and time of day, I'll phone you. Then we can drive up together. It's just south of West Point, if you remember. Okay?"

Chris: "Okay. We'll talk later."

*   *   *

A week later the two were driving up along the west bank of the Hudson River, still considered America's Rhine. Verne had them both settled aboard his restored car, a "Spacemobile," a real antique, but updated and running smoothly. When they had gone almost as far as Port Montgomery, they turned left off the main highway and went along a long or private corporate drive. Chris admired the old and imposing Lombardy poplars that lined the drive, relieved here and there with plashing fountains. Like everything else in sight, the architects had designed the fancy birthday-cake fountains in high Art Deco style from the long-ago 1920s and 1930s.

At last the gigantic headquarters building loomed ahead, much less in height but more in rounded mass, a real Art Deco masterpiece that always impressed the visitor, no matter how often it was observed. The chief building did in fact resemble the giant birthday cake to which people usually compared it.

Verne stopped at the imposing and grandiose gatehouse. One of the guards on duty checked Verne's, and no less Chris's credentials, and then waved them on. They parked to one side of the main entrance, a little distance away, in a special parking space reserved for important visitors or employees. Verne had somehow finagled it. Chris was impressed in spite of himself.

"Good show, Verne," he quipped, and then observed, "Negotiating or navigating ashore, as opposed to doing this in outer space, appears to require almost as much finesse, but of a different kind." Verne laughed in response, as they made their entrance into the cavernous lobby of the Outer Space Consortium. At least plenty of light, natural or manmade, flooded the interior.

They went up to the central counter. Verne gave his name to one of the people on duty there. A beautiful young lady smiled and said, "I'll take you two to the office where you have the appointment."

She sat them down in the outer office while she talked with the secretary on duty that day. As their lovely cicerone left to return to the lobby, she said, "All is in order. The secretary will escort you into the inner office in just a few minutes."

Chris: "So who is this mighty muck-a-muck who will interview us about our special request?"

Verne: "The assistant CEO himself."

When Chris registered his astonishment, Verne advised him, "Don't be too impressed. We went to school together, high school and then college."

A male secretary escorted them into the inner office. There a tall and authoritative-looking man sat behind an old-fashioned mahogany desk, a large and formidable barrier. He got up and approached them, smiling broadly.

"Verne, how are you?" The two embraced. Then Verne introduced him to Chris as Amicus Jones.

The assistant CEO had them sit in the two chairs facing his desk, and then he returned to his own chair, reshuffling some papers before him.

Amicus: "We have here your special request for both of you, together, to move on from transfer ship duty to function as captain and chief navigator on a cruise liner, but not going beyond our galaxy. I must say that you have both achieved an excellent service record aboard the transfer giants. Something like twenty years each. That includes the needed time off between voyages."

Amicus looked up from the papers before him on the desk. Verne and then Chris palavered with him for several minutes. The assistant CEO grinned at them. "I see no major problem why we can't accede to your request. You both have a long paid vacation that's now your legal due per contract. That will give us plenty of time to arrange the transfer from garbage scow to cruise liner. Oh, before I forget: you will both have to take a few classes in the proper decorum for officers aboard the interstellar liners. You'll have to deal with the public. Understood?"

Verne and Chris nodded back at him. Amicus looked at his watch. "Ah, it's almost lunchtime. We have a very good cafeteria here for the company officers. That includes all three of us. Why don't you come along with me as my guests?" Again the two smiled and nodded back.

In addition to the headquarters up the Hudson, the Outer Space Consortium occupied the first three floors of the ancient but still magnificent Chrysler Building. On the third floor, in an old but refurbished office, the corporation had set up classrooms for special instruction, including the Public Decorum Curriculum that Chris and Verne were taking. Almost six months had gone by since their interview with Amicus Jones not far southeast of Port Montgomery. During the last month of their six-month vacation Amicus had arranged for captain and chief navigator to attend the classes conveniently located in Manhattan, where they still maintained their regular homes, both in the village at the south of the island.

After class one day, the brief course of study nearing its end,

Chris and Verne adjourned to one of the cocktail bars that the corporation had so thoughtfully installed on each floor. They were both nursing a margarita, plus nibbling on a mild Mexican-style dip with crunchy toasted tortilla chips.

Chris: "Well, Verne, are you learning from these, ahem, sensitivity classes?"

Verne: "To tell the truth, I'm learning or relearning quite a bit. I don't feel superior to this instruction, by the way. And you?"

Chris: "At first I found it all pretty obvious, but now I've changed my mind. It's all useful, and will be even more so once we're back on ship." He paused. "I think these classes apply more to you than to me, you as the captain, the CEO aboard ship. As chief navigator, unless I mingle in uniform with the passengers whenever I'm on duty in public, I won't see that much of them." He looked up acutely toward Verne.

The captain spoke. "It isn't that the customers, the passengers, are always right, but they are all paying a helluva lotta money to travel on these exotic voyages, even if the trips don't generally last more than four to six months."

Chris nodded at him, before Verne continued. "I heard from Amicus last night. He phoned me on his own time. He has found us both a suitable berth together on one of the best cruise liners, and in our usual occupations. These liners specialize in exotic interstellar trips. In our case we will embark on the special Robinson Crusoe Tour. Although we'll stop at various planets, we'll sojourn at one in particular, where the company stages a fake but seemingly real Robinson Crusoe adventure. Depending on circumstances, we'll be gone half a year."

Chris: "Robinson Crusoe? It sounds promising but perhaps

also a little ominous. When do we go up to Alphabet for a look-see at the liner? What is it called?"

Verne: "You won't believe this, but shades of the old *Star Trek* series, it's called the U.S.S.S. *Enterprise!* Amicus has scheduled our look-see for next week." Of course, Verne had no need to explain that the initials stood for United States Star Ship, but pronouncing the initials deliberately made it sound all the more official. Verne winked at Chris.

Chris: "You can give me the relevant particulars later. I'm going home. We'll see each other next week."

They both stood up, embraced, and left the bar and then the building at the same time.

Everything proceeded in due order and according to schedule. On the day before the take-off from the Big Home Harbor, everyone involved had made everything ready to go. The officers, the crew, the service people (many people were needed to run and maintain the vessel), and in particular the passengers had all come aboard the colossal space liner and had settled in their respective quarters, or in the case of the crew and service people, in their working areas. All the personnel had everything in order and under control, apart from the new employees (mostly graduates just out of space school or academy) who were embarking on their very first voyage into outer space.

Verne settled in as captain, and so did Chris as chief navigator, sharing the same working area, the so-called bridge, located as usual in the upper and forward part of the starship, a wide and capacious chamber. They had both come aboard a few days earlier than anyone else, apart from the service people. They had both gone over much of the liner with its multiple spaces and levels.

Captain and crew had checked everything: all was ready to go for take-off. Apart from fuel (the first thing taken aboard and properly secured), the crew and service people had brought on ship all the important supplies, especially the food, the water, the beverages—in short, the provisions of all types—and for the passengers a gigantic amount of alcohol of all kinds, beer, wine, liqueurs, hard liquor—you name it, they had it all in place. The sheer weight of the people and provisions proved enormous, but the starship could easily accommodate and transport them all.

At long last the day of the big departure had arrived. The starship, it was confirmed, would be gone around six months, barring unforeseen accidents, mishaps, et alia. As ever the ship had its full complement of medical people, whether doctors, nurses, or all the medical personnel required for such a large starship and such a relatively long voyage. The regular personnel and the passengers felt perfectly confident about the safety and security of the space liner and its itinerary.

For Verne and Chris it boded well that Amicus had found for them such a fun and exciting trip as the Robinson Crusoe Tour. They thanked him profusely, and when he came to see them off, they treated him to a fine dinner and then to a new musical comedy on Broadway. So far their shift in professional occupation had worked out with amazing suavity. They felt lucky and even thrilled. Off the starship went on its voyage to the other side of the galaxy, our galaxy, the one we call the Milky Way.

Across the bridge they grinned at each other.

IV. Up, Off, and Away

Its red and emerald beacons from the night
Draw human moths in melancholy flight,
With beams whose gaudy glories point the way
To safety or destruction—choose who may!
        George Sterling, "The Apothecary's" (quite a trip!)

For this voyage the giant space liner was not using the M.S.D., or Maximum Super Drive, generally deployed for trips beyond our galaxy. Operating as they were just inside the Milky Way, the ship used only the older and still adequate Super Drive. They still made very good time. Only a few days out from the Big Home Harbor the starship had already crossed a significant amount of distance to the first planets at which they would stop. Even if it always appeared artificial at first to those traveling in space on their first occasion, the ship maintained the daily twenty-four-hour schedule that had become the normal routine back on Mother Earth. Their bodies remained Earth-bodies.

Chris talking quietly with Verne on the bridge: "I'll see you tonight at the captain's table, or at that of the officers? Nice choice we always have!"

Verne: "No, tonight I eat in my own quarters, if you'd like to join me there. Space liner decorum and protocol advise us to eat in uniform out in the big main dining hall more often than not. It makes for easy socializing between passengers and ship's personnel. But we can still take the occasional, and private, meal in our quarters, if so we wish. No?"

Chris nodded: "A definite yes! I'll join you at our usual time, 7:30 or so." They nodded in agreement.

They met as agreed in the captain's unusually spacious and luxurious quarters for drinks and eats. They were off shift.

Chris: "Well, the Outer Space Consortium certainly does things up fine and dandy on these outer space liners. I'm still impressed, in particular after our adequate but relatively spartan accommodations in the supercargo space ships, our transfer giants. How do you find it? What do you think?"

Verne: "In certain respects it is much better, and it is much easier. We have more help, more officers, than on a transfer giant. Socially, however, it is demanding. The frequent need to meet and speak with people, passengers above all, keeps me on my toes. And on my most cheerful behavior."

Chris: "I agree, but I need to circulate much less than you as captain. If I do mingle, it's on my own time when I'm out of uniform. I've already met a number of suitable mamzelles my own age. Some *are* looking for a shipboard romance. I'm willing to grant their wishes."

Verne: "You are taking the usual precautions?"

Chris: "I'm honest, but only tell them that I'm part of the service personnel behind the scenes. Not a lie. In a sense that is true. Let's see how my first affair on board proceeds! Oh yes, if it leads to real intimacy, heavy-duty emotional, I have my supply of official forms for them to read and sign."

He was not referring to birth control, but he did not have to explain the reference. It had long since become firm protocol that, if a passenger became involved with a crew member, and if things did not turn out well—barring pregnancy, of course, if it involved a woman—the ship and consortium were not liable in any lawsuit because of some emotional imbroglio. Passengers proceeded at their own risk, but with birth control for men and women both, no need to worry.

Verne: "I assume you have studied our itinerary relative to our planetary stops. Yes?"

Chris: "Yes, of course. We'll be stopping at a series of Earth-like planets in different solar systems. Some already very close to Earth, and others have been Terra-formed to make them comfortable and healthy for us human primates. The chief animals are not primates and pose no threat to our domination, or to us personally—proceeding with due caution.

"We have long since established colonies on them with our ever-increasing human populations. The basic economy on them all is agriculture and basic sustenance, however small the populations are at the moment. These planets are all doing well. Their natural flora and fauna, as well as their beauty, suffice for the time being. Correct?"

Verne smiled. "Yes, I see that you have read with care the materials that the consortium has furnished us. Good! *The* Robinson Crusoe planet, however, is a semitropical paradise, and the largest of them all: jungle, mountains, and oceans with many islands, oceans that encircle the planet. Let's see how it goes." They smiled at each other.

The U.S.S.S. *Enterprise* stopped in due course at the several planets before the big one, where the consortium staged the fake but apparently genuine Robinson Crusoe adventure. (Nobody seemed concerned about the genuine quality of it, or about any real danger that the adventure might engender.) Wherever they stopped, the fleet of small space dories would take any passengers who so wished to visit that particular world. They always went with guides and guards to protect them just in case. But for the Robinson Crusoe planet, where almost all the passengers were planning to disembark, a virtual army would accompany them, many guards in virtual disguise. The consortium could not afford to let the passengers go wandering around without protection or due caution.

The giant space liner had at last reached RCP 100, and had positioned itself into orbit around it. Tomorrow morning the advance crew would go down to the surface of this world twice as large as Earth. They would land in their small spacecraft at the chief station where the regular planet personnel was waiting to greet them. Per advance communication, all was in order, all was ready.

That evening, once again, neither captain nor chief navigator ate out in the main dining hall, but once again in the privacy of the captain's quarters.

Verne: "Here we are at last. I'm content to eat here with you. We need not be on guard for crew or passenger. We can relax by ourselves, and say what we want without worrying."

Chris: "I like eating in the main dining hall well enough—that's what we do for the most part—but to eat here out of public scrutiny *is* an agreeable change, yes! To shift the subject, you are not going down with the advance crew, right?"

Verne: "Correct. I'll descend on the day following tomorrow; that is when you can come along, if you want."

Chris: "Yes, I do. I'm eager to see what this more spectacular planet Earth looks like and feels like up close. The other navigators can take care of the ship, with the captain's permission, that is." Here he winked at Verne, then continued. "How lucky for us, for everyone, that RCP 100 has an atmosphere like Mother Earth's!" He looked acutely at the captain.

Verne: "You said it! Also that it is relatively free of dangerous insects or hostile animals. All the personnel that have rotated here report that this world is comparatively safe, with all due caution observed.

"We've already checked everything out by regular communication with people on the planet, but spacecraft protocol stipulates that, once we reach our destination in planetary orbit, we also do so in person. Who knows what's hidden underground?

"But the usual undercover army will go out in disguise and in full force during the first and biggest embarkation of the passengers. Everything reportedly has been prepared for them. Enough! Let's watch an old movie."

The advance team of engineers and scientists had gone down to the planet's surface, and all was well, or so they reported when they returned on the evening of their descent. All boded well for the captain's own descent on the morrow, as required by legal protocol. Verne was a stickler for laws and customs. To this he owed his eminence as captain, as well as to his excellent record as a commander.

Like every first visitor to RCP 100, everyone in the captain's party registered amazement and wonder at the chief hotel or headquarters. It was gigantic, even larger than the space liner, and much more like an enormous ocean cruiser back on Earth, even if sited in the midst of semiformal gardens on a very large, flat-topped hill. Whoever had laid it out had the giant Art Deco cruise liners of the American 1930s in mind as the model.

Even if all the people in the captain's group had seen it on their p.c.'s, as well as their hand-held devices, the sheer size of the building turned it into a source of astonishment. Chris could not help but compare his own surprise to what he had felt when he first visited Egypt and the chief ancient sites there. Photos or films could not capture the visceral feeling on getting up close to such oversized monuments.

While visiting on the planet, above all in the semitropical zone (warm but not overly so), the passengers would have a great place to stay, and a great base for trips of discovery and exploration. Everyone noted with wry humor that the architect had named the hotel the U.S. Shipwreck *Robinson Crusoe*.

The caretaker staff greeted the newcomers in the main lobby, and with extra warmth. Smiling broadly, their urbane leader shook the hands of everyone in the captain's party. "Welcome to RCP 100! May you have a grand visit while staying here! Welcome! We shall do our all to help you."

The captain repeated in person what he had already told them by wireless telephone. The space liner would begin landing the passengers tomorrow morning either via the squadron of space dories or (unusually) via a spectacular but officially approved "shipwreck." The big starship would make a landing in or on the ocean about a mile offshore from the hotel. The captain requested a fleet of large motorboats to ferry passengers and their luggage to the giant guesthouse.

Such an unorthodox landing was perfectly safe and possible, even if it meant a colossal effort to get the starship back into outer space, after the extended sojourn.

Chris could not help quipping to the caretaker leader, "Some shipwreck you have here, the most luxurious I could imagine!" They grinned at each other. Soon the captain and the caretaker leader had arranged everything between them. The spacecraft party returned to the *Enterprise,* to prepare for the big landing tomorrow, the space liner's foothold in space, only this time in inner space.

V. A Foothold on RCP 100

That evening, the one before the scheduled landing on the next day, the captain briefly held forth via the loudspeaker system. Unless in an emergency, the system only worked in the big public areas of the starship, the main dining halls, the smaller eateries, and other public spaces, including the chief lobby, where many people gathered just to hang out.

"As announced earlier, we wish to remind the passengers and personnel that our scheduled landing will begin at 9 A.M. Please have your luggage ready to go. We have decided to land our space liner on the ocean only a mile or so offshore from the hotel or headquarters where we shall all be staying as our base while on this new planet. This landing, even if unorthodox, is not unprecedented, and is perfectly safe. Let everyone be reassured of that. We shall all see everyone again at breakfast. Get a good night's rest."

Chris had listened with particular acuteness. It devolved upon him as the chief navigator to handle the descent to the planet's surface and then onto the ocean, where the starship would rest at anchor more or less. Meanwhile the caretaker crew would remain aboard until relieved by other crew members on the planet.

Everyone was agog, of course, to disembark on the new planet of spectacular beauty and variety twice the size of Mother Earth, and in a locale of great physical comfort, semi-tropical, and not prone to storm, earthquake, or too much rain.

Thanks to Chris and his fellow navigators, the *Enterprise* made a very smooth descent the next morning, spiralling ever downward and landing on the surface of the ocean as planned. The captain complimented all on such a suave transition. As soon as the ocean calmed from the massive displacement caused by the landing in the necessarily deep water, and not far off-shore, a large flotilla of motorboats arrived alongside the huge space liner. They began ferrying the people and their gear on-shore, where another fleet but of regular land vehicles then took them to the U.S. Shipwreck *Robinson Crusoe*. Getting everyone transported and settled in their new quarters required most of that daytime and the early evening, even with the army of people assisting them. But at last everyone had gotten settled in their new spaces in the hotel—the passengers, the spacecraft crew, and miscellaneous personnel. Everyone would meet at dinner in the vast indoor chamber of the chief eatery, also employed for general assembly.

That night, mid-evening, later than usual due to the circumstances of the disembarkation—the semi-tropical sunset overwhelmed all the newcomers—speaking from the captain's table while holding a cordless microphone, the caretaker leader at the hotel addressed all the people present from off the starship, quite a number.

"Welcome to all of you disembarking from the U.S.S.S. *Enterprise*. We, the caretakers of this hotel, our planetary headquarters, are here to help and guide and guard you. Although this is a fairly gentle planet—free of other primates as far as we know, but with some ferocious species of wildlife—we counsel you to go about your discovering and exploration with due care and caution. Go forth in groups of some size, with weapons of self-defense, or best of all with armed guards from your spacecraft. If you do go forth on your own, as you know according to the papers that you have signed, the Outer Space Consortium takes no responsibility. Apart from this advice or admonition, we can only welcome you here on RCP 100. Speaking personally, we caretaker folk are quite content to see so many new faces. Welcome, and welcome again and again!"

The caretaker leader had exuded a special warmth while speaking, and the entire dinner assemblage of people applauded and cheered. Everyone was eager to see what tomorrow would bring, and equally eager to explore the new planet.

By mid-morning everyone and everything seemed ready to tackle the great outdoors. Although the captain remained in command, he let the caretaker leader, Dion Ombray, take over for the first few days. The latter addressed everyone still sitting at the tables in the enormous eating or assembly hall. Everyone had eaten, and the service personnel had cleared the breakfast dishes and cleaned the tables.

"First, we are all on a first-name basis here. Speaking for myself, as the hotel caretaker leader, as well as for our staff, welcome again to RCP 100! Today is your first day of exploration, and we ask you that you do not go too far away. Concentrate on the immediate vicinity, the gardens and the parklike areas just beyond them or into the nearest woods. Maybe a little beyond the farms that produce the fruits and vegetables for our headquarters here.

"Please go in groups and with the guards who carry weapons. You may encounter some ferocious specimen of wildlife. The latter is not likely. Since we established ourselves and the farms, the feral birds and animals have abandoned our region and somewhat beyond. They in turn take no chances with us in the same way as we with them. You'll have many pleasant surprises. Have a great first outing. We'll see each other tonight at dinner, when I'll be happy to hear your reactions and any questions you might have by then."

Once outdoors, the first thing the newcomers noticed: how similar everything appeared to the semi-tropical climate back on Earth. Here flourished trees and plants like those in the Caribbean, but with very high mountains at a great distance inland almost like the Himalayas. A sample of the typical comments made by the passengers: "This is almost like the West Indies!" "What lush greenery! We might just as well be visiting Cuba, Hispaniola, or Jamaica." "We've gone to the other side of our galaxy only to find what looks like our home planet." "Amazing, even the trees and plants look like those on Earth." "These could be palm trees. Those could be orchids. And look at the big flame-colored birds squawking and sitting up on those monster trees that look like banyans."

Some passengers commented on this astonishing similarity to the caretaker guides among them, and asked them about it. Most of the guides answered in the same way.

"You ask how this could have happened. We can only invoke various recondite laws or principles. Cosmic Coincidence, Cosmic Duplication, or Cosmic Reduplication. However we explain it, or can't explain it, it is a scientific fact."

Because of the similarity, a few passengers expressed a minor disappointment. The guides then responded. "Let's see what you have to say after we continue exploring in the next few days. Today we hike, but once we get beyond easy reach of the hotel, we'll be taking you in vehicles to the new locations. And from there we'll hike to nearby points. We'll bring our picnic lunches with us, as we are doing today."

By the time that everyone returned to the hotel, it was mid-afternoon. Nobody was complaining about any disappointment. Nonetheless, after the evening meal Dion Ombray had enough to do, fielding the comments and questions from the passengers as they came up to him at his table to speak with him personally. Almost invariably he finished by saying, "Let's see what tomorrow brings!" He said the same thing to Chris and Verne when they came up to him. Tomorrow they would go out with everyone else, even if Dion remained nominally in charge.

VI. An Outing and Several Encounters

In fact, on the very next day Chris and Verne along with others would observe what the morrow might bring. They consulted with Dion before the expedition during the second day on the new and amazing planet. Dion spoke: "We do not know how the individual specimens of wildlife will respond to our expedition members. This includes above all the passengers, even if attended by the guards in disguise or not. But let us not assume antagonistic or life-threatening encounters as deriving from the members of unknown species. Let us assume that we can avoid combative meetings between us and the native entities here, but just in case we must remain on guard."

Dion smiled at Verne and Chris, and the three of them embraced. Verne reassured their local guide and leader, "Yes, I am the captain and nominally in charge, but in case of an emergency let's work, you and I, hand in hand. Okay?" Dion signified by nodding that he found the partnership to his liking.

Verne: "That being the case, I'll tag along with you, staying not far from you with other guides and guards."

The fleet of tough and all-purpose vehicles arrived, and everyone climbed aboard. Off the expedition went, onward into unknown regions. Everyone had a sense of caution, but unprecedentedly with little fear. The sense of comfortable adventure prevailed. The beauty of the new planet promised both happy discovery and exploration.

That morning at breakfast the captain had reminded everyone over the loudspeaker system to exercise due care and caution. "If you separate yourself from your group somehow and face what looks like an unfriendly entity, don't panic. Don't run. If you can, climb calmly up a nearby and climbable tree. Via your hand-held device call us. We'll come to your rescue as soon as possible."

Chris would likewise tag along with Verne, close to Dion with other guides and guards. Better safe than sorry! After the fleet of vehicles drove off, Dion in the advance one spoke over the loudspeaker system interconnecting the vehicles. Both Verne and Chris paid acute attention to what Dion had to say.

"We'll be driving somewhat beyond the farms that supply our headquarters. You'll note some small but real differences between the verdure around the hotel and what we'll soon see. The difference is intentional: we wanted to make our initial environment as Earth-like as possible, to reassure you, our guests, as much as we could. Soon you'll see mixed blue-green and purple-green foliage. Some species of trees and plants are gigantic. You'll see jungle-like areas startlingly distinct from what you may know of those on Earth.

"Similarly, some of the wildlife resembling what you may have encountered in the Congo or the Amazon will seem twice as large, including lion-like and elephant-like species among others. We call the big lion-like creatures the megavores, and they are indeed carnivorous. We have lost no human to them as of yet, be reassured. For the giant elephant-like creatures we use the older medieval term of ollyphant, as christened by one of our more erudite scientists.

"Once we park all our vehicles in the large open space a real distance beyond the farmland, we'll get out. From that spot we can all radiate out in smaller groups. You will be on your own along with others, but please be careful not to stray too far from your particular group. We cannot guarantee your safety otherwise."

The vehicles reached the wide glade as described, and everyone disembarked. They formed into small groups, each one with guides and guards. Off they went, hiking here and there. Chris and Verne tagged along with the group headed by Dion. Wisely everyone wore the stout boot-like coverings for the legs that Dion had strongly recommended, and that the hotel furnished. These would protect the legs from anything untoward, whether plant or animal or insect, that might pose a threat from ground level. Again Chris thought to himself: *Better safe than sorry!* Verne and he had visited too many alien planets not to respect the wisdom in that folk saying.

Chris had almost no sense of genuine fear, but he did not need to act stupidly to appreciate due care and caution. Early in his life he had to learn the hard way without too much damage about the worth of caution when in endangered circumstances. Somehow or other he had separated himself, but not far, from Dion's group. He did carry atomic weaponry, which he would use only in an extreme emergency.

He had no desire to kill any member of an alien form of animal life. He might not have hesitated to kill a very large insect. He wandered down an avenue of huge fern-like plants with giant fronds. This avenue gave way to one lined with equally large trees that debouched into a large glade. The avenue continued on the other side opposite from where Chris had paused. He was about to turn back to join the others, but something stopped him. A premonition maybe.

All at once a monstrous creature emerged from that other opening. Although with his attention acutely focussed, Chris oddly felt almost no fear. He stood as motionless and self-contained as he could hold himself, even if his heart did beat much faster than usual.

The creature was as magnificent a specimen of a megavore as anyone could imagine, like an African lion only twice the size, perhaps even larger. The animal advanced slowly toward Chris, but seemed to hide no antagonism or anything threatening. What majesty, what dignity!

Despite his much smaller size Chris appeared to fascinate the megavore as much as the megavore transfixed the human. Nor did the lion-like creature seem to be hungry, as he had already eaten his first kill of the day. The entity stopped in front of Chris and proceeded to look at him keenly, in the same way that Chris looked back at him. Then with his enormous nose the megavore bent his head downward and began sniffing him all over. All of a sudden the creature extruded an enormous purple tongue and licked him on the head, almost covering it, as if perhaps in blessing, and then withdrew the tongue back into his maw. Bizarrely, the megavore's breath did not seem foul but heavy and sweet.

Now Chris in his turn held one of the giant front paws, be-furred and heavily clawed, between his hands, but not moving it otherwise. Next he bent down and planted a firm kiss thereupon. This gesture seemed to surprise and please the lion-like creature almost as much as his licking of the human's head had pleased Chris. Chris then backed off and bowed to the megavore. He turned around and slowly walked away with as much dignity and majesty as the megavore had shown when advancing toward him.

Without too much delay Chris found his way back to Dion's group, which was slowly moving away in a different direction. Apparently no one had noticed the navigator's absence, so absorbed was everyone in looking around at their novel surroundings. For the time being Chris kept his unique adventure to himself, even as he stayed thrilled to his core by this encounter. Later, when alone with Verne, he would tell his tale.

Along with others in Dion's group, Verne stood in a narrow path or clearing between gigantic bushes with purple furry leaves. Everyone was fixedly staring at what seemed like extra-large orchids. To Chris they looked like exotic goblin faces. In fact they were not really epiphytes like those back on Earth at all. The resemblance was pure coincidence like so much else on RCP 100. Nonetheless, they exerted a curious fascination. Beyond the path between the huge floral bushes there stretched a broad grassy plain. About a mile or less to the north a high grassy ridge blocked the horizon, to which everyone turned, and began walking out on the plain.

Chris went up to Verne, and spoke very low: "Did you miss me?" Verne: "Why, were you gone?" Chris: "I wandered off a bit by myself, and had a thrilling but not lethal encounter. I'll tell you tonight when we're alone in your official quarters at the hotel." Verne smiled: "Fine, I'm eager to hear it! Meanwhile Dion tells us that the group here will soon have a thrilling encounter of our own. He expects a herd to come up over the ridge just there to the north." He pointed at the elevation.

The whole group stood still, speaking quietly among themselves. Suddenly all along the central part of the ridge a herd of quadrupeds with grey but unfurred hide came up. They did resemble elephants, and came to rest briefly on the flat level at the top. The ollyphants riveted everyone's attention. Enormous, twice the size of the African elephant, they began majestically and slowly moving forward across the plain toward the small group of humans.

Dion advised, "Just continue standing, and make no abrupt movements." Then he picked up his wireless phone out of his right pocket, dialed, and spoke: "Send some of the vans to pick us up as soon as possible." He gave the coordinates for their location. In truth both Dion's group and the vans were not that far from each other.

Soon enough, the open-air vans arrived, and Dion had everyone get into them. He spoke, "We'll sit here until the ollyphants are almost close enough to charge. I doubt that they will. Still, we don't want a massacre of us underneath their ponderous feet!" Everyone smiled, and nodded.

The beasts had gigantic tusks, huge trunks, and titanic flapping ears. Their eyes appeared tiny by comparison like those of African elephants. Everyone could feel the heavy vibrations produced by the weight of the ponderous animals. Their sheer size alone gave everyone a genuine moment of awe and near terror. They had come close enough. Dion gave the signal, and the vans drove off back to where the vans had first reconnoitered, or disembarked. Everyone gave a huge sigh of relief. The beasts had not charged, and had not followed the vans. They continued moving south to where the humans had paused.

The other groups had reconvened, and Dion advised the other drivers to return everyone back to the headquarters. It was not that late, maybe midafternoon, but it was time to go back. Everyone had their fill of exotic excitement for that day at least.

Late afternoon until early evening, almost everyone had gathered in the vast indoor chamber, where most people ate unless they ate in their private rooms or suites courtesy of room service. On this occasion the passengers had convened for a general assembly. Before convening, most of the assemblage had showered, and had garbed them in casual attire. Ostensibly they had all come together for the ship's (the hotel's) happy hour, and to exchange stories and impressions.

Keeping a safe distance, some guests had encountered very large animals that resembled certain Earth-like species but almost always twice as large. These were species like lions, tigers, elephants (the same ollyphants that came near Dion and his group), hippopotami, giraffes, and many others, but all distinct from those that the passengers remembered from Earth's tropical and semitropical regions.

Some guests had identified what they thought big rodents. They turned out to be giant rodent-like insects, more than fearsome because of their size. The humans had sagely stayed away from them. The entities had bitten or attacked no one. They seemed to have formidable teeth and claws. No guests even thought of disobeying the counsel of the guides and guards. Nobody wanted to be injured because of rash or foolhardy behavior, inviting alien wounds and alien infection.

Even if the medical staff at the hotel or from the starship could surely handle a wide range of medical problems, limits and limitations existed beyond which the medical people might not be able to bring relief or remedy. Still, as Dion reminded the assembled guests and personnel, accidents would happen. Once again he warned them to keep on guard with all due care and caution. He hoped that they were indeed enjoying the novel sights and sounds, particularly the singing of the exotic birds.

Meanwhile, before they joined the general assembly, Verne and Chris imbibed each a cocktail in the captain's quarters. They had both showered, and had changed their uniforms. The navigator related to Verne his encounter with the giant lion-like creature. Verne: "That was amazing and scary. You were lucky. He could just as easily have detached your head. No bad effects from his saliva?" Chris: "No problem. As I walked away, I wiped my head with my heavy-duty handkerchief. I washed my head and hair when I showered." He added, "I've always had a fantastic immune system!"

Verne smiled, "Don't push your luck, but let's go downstairs for the general assembly, even if we are off-duty. I want to hear other people's reactions, and learn what Master Dion has in store for us tomorrow. Then we can eat and confer. I can't speak for you, but I plan to go to bed early tonight." Chris: "Me, too! Let's go downstairs."

*   *   *

Entering late, they sat down at the back of the gathering, just as Dion was finishing up his after-the-expedition spiel. "So, dear compadres in adventure, that's the line-up for the day after tomorrow. Instead of us all going to a common point, and radiating out from there, we'll form into two dozen groups heading in different directions for different locales. You'll find the two dozen spots listed on your phones. Check the list out. Tomorrow we remain here, in and around the hotel, while we organize the expeditions.

"Because it's possible that circumstances might make the individual outings last longer than a day, we'll make sure in advance you'll have plenty of supplies with you, drink and food above all, of course. The last supply ships that arrived, they came before you did, left us with enormous quantities of everything that we might need on our next expeditions. For some of the more distant locales we'll use the smaller spacecraft rather than the all-purpose vans.

"We'll give you more information and instructions tomorrow. As for me I'm taking my own group to a special spot by the seashore. That's all for now."

VII. Expeditiously, Expeditionly

Beauty, what dost thou here?

Why hauntest thou this empery of pain

Where men in vain

Long for another sphere?

"An Altar of the West," George Sterling.

(Point Lobos . . . Carmel Bay.)

The next day, expeditiously, Dion Ombray and his own staff resident in the hotel-headquarters, together with advice from the captain and his chief navigator, planned the two dozen expeditions patiently and systematically. They all worked closely with the passengers to satisfy the latter's preferences.

Surprisingly, about half a dozen different groups, including Dion's own, opted for the seashore and, if prudent and/or feasible, for the ocean with diving and swimming. Even if spread out along an extended piece of beach or other shore, everyone would remain in touch via the telephone and intercom provided by their hand-held devices.

Another half-dozen groups would go by van to the moderately distant open plain and foothills of the first range of the mountains visible from the hotel, thirty or forty miles to the north. Yet another half-dozen groups would visit the range of mountains beyond those visible from the hotel. Still another half-dozen groups would go by small spacecraft or aircraft to the mountains almost half-around the planet. All these destinations appeared as viable choices in case any untoward situation or problem might arise. No one was anticipating any difficulties that had not already happened under Dion's direction. The different groups would take their collective leave around midmorning the next day.

When Dion and his own group arrived at the seashore a little after midmorning, Verne and Chris like all the others opened their eyes even wider. They noted how much like a seashore on Mother Planet Earth it seemed. Smooth sand, some big shells here and there, and even large rock formations every now and then. What a big and agreeable surprise!

The water seemed warmer than cold or cool. Some passengers doffed their outer garments, but had already put on their swimsuits underneath. They waded into the water, and began swimming. Dion shouted, reminding them, "Don't go too far out!"

Just beyond a rock formation an older man encountered a giant jellyfish. but the latter seemed curious, and advanced toward him. Before he could swim away, the jellyfish had reached him. The swimmer could not avoid contact, and received such a powerful shock of electricity that he had time only to scream for help, and then he passed out.

The jellyfish retreated, but other swimmers came to his rescue, and brought him to shore, inert. With Chris and Verne helping out, they managed to resuscitate him. The older man seemed to be okay, once he recovered. But he had endured a strong and nasty shock. At Dion's command a van arrived, and took the man back to the hotel for medical examination, but apart from the shock he appeared alright.

Meanwhile Dion continued his presentation, pointing out the similarities and the differences between this environment and the one back on Earth. "The cephalopods, whether squids or octopi, are gigantic. Don't go exploring any underwater caverns, especially the bigger ones, where they like to lair. We may not see you again if you do swim in those caves."

Around noon everyone moved somewhat inland of the beach, and retired behind a hedge of palm trees, some tall, but most of them rounded and shorter. Here in a kind of glade they sat down, and ate their prepared lunches. Dion advised, "Save the lunch containers; we can re-use them. Chris and Verne sat next to him, and they palavered on this and that.

Verne enquired of Dion, "Since you and the staff are more or less permanently employed here, what do you do for love-life? That is, if I might be so bold as to ask." He smiled as he spoke. Dion smiled back.

"Since you ask, let me speak openly. Some of us have lovers among our own ranks, that is, among the staff. We also have a number of professional escorts, as we prefer the term. Some, the specialists, have their own special workplaces, as apart from their chambers. Some of them are an authorized part of the staff who pick up extra money or credits this way."

Chris grinned as he spoke. "I'd like to sample their wares, or rather their skills, if not priced exorbitantly." Dion replied, "You and the escort would arrange that between you. Do you have a preference as to gender?" Chris thought a moment before he spoke. "Usually female, but maybe I'd like to try both. I'm curious about this escort service, especially what it might involve for a male."

Dion: "Very well. When we return to the hotel, I'll give you a list of names and phone numbers, plus other specific data. It is up to you to initiate the connection. The staff, including myself, do not make the arrangements." Dion smiled amicably, and stood up, speaking in a big booming voice.

"Let's return to the beach! We'll head back to the hotel around midafternoon."

The hotel spokesman continued his presentation at the seashore. A little before midafternoon, everyone felt a curious but powerful turbulence, like a wind that one could feel but whose effects one could not easily see. It lasted several minutes, and proved so violent that several people collapsed but did not fall into unconsciousness. However, everyone had felt this unseen wind.

Dion spoke again. "Let's everyone return to the hotel. Help your neighbors to manoeuvre if they are having trouble walking."

The unseen turbulence had thrown their phones that everyone carried out of order, as the passengers and staff soon discovered. What could that turbulence mean? Dion simply said, "I'll explain what has happened, but the phenomenon is rare, have no fear."

VIII. Momentous Pause

Crisis. Chaos. Emergency.

All these terms along with other thoughts ran through everyone's head as they walked back to the hotel-headquarters. A thrill of adventure coursed through everyone. Dion merely smiled amiably, and continued to reassure his overall group. Verne and Chris followed his example, both garbed casually. A few of the other outing parties had already returned.

Dion waited until the overall seashore groups had also come back. Most people had reassembled in the great chamber where most of them ate. The electronic equipment in the hotel still functioned, a real mercy. Over the loud-speaker and intercom system, he summoned everyone to the great assembly room, apart from those on duty, but everyone in the hotel could hear him.

"Attention, everyone! While most of us here were having our outing by the beach, and elsewhere, an unusually powerful electrical storm developed on and in the sun that illuminates this solar system, including RCP 100. These storms rarely happen, and rarely disturb our electronic devices and features in the hotel. They all have a safety feature engineered in them. But the feature does not necessarily extend to our hand-held and other smaller devices. Everything can be corrected, although it will take time. We can then engineer the same feature in our personal phones and computers."

Dion had paused while he looked around over the assembly, and kept on smiling before speaking again.

"These electrical storms happen so seldom that we overlooked warning you about them. It is our own responsibility, or my own, and I confess the failure. I am less concerned about the groups that did not go far, but am concerned about those on the other side of the planet. Others are now trying to contact them. We'll see what happens, but there's no reason for panic. Most of you people signed up for the promise of adventure, and we are having one.

"I shall remain in place here to answer your questions and concerns, and receive your brickbats and criticisms. Thank you, and remember, no need to panic."

Dion had spoken from a kind of rostrum while standing at the head table. He then sat down, but continued to smile, and project good cheer in his accustomed reassuring manner. Verne and Chris were sitting next to him, while all three consulted with each other.

They both asked the same question, one after another. "What about the space ship?" Dion answered forthrightly: "You told me it is a new ship. The safety feature should be built in, but to be sure have one of the navigators on board check it out."

By midevening, despite the handicap of the failed electronics, all the other expeditions had returned.

As they came back, they assembled and ate in the largest chamber of the hotel-headquarters, or the H. H. Q., as people now termed it, thus abbreviated for convenience. The others who had already assembled and eaten awaited and welcomed them.

For the first time it was Captain Verne Laverne who spoke from the rostrum at the head table, looking out over the sea of faces. He had already consulted with Dion as to what to say, to emphasize, and with a great big reassuring smile.

"Greetings to all of you! Congratulations on having an exceptional outing! You have all returned safe and sound! Dion with his own group—which included your captain and chief navigator—had the one casualty, a passenger. A big jellyfish touched and somewhat electrocuted him, but he survived and is well, still with us."

Here the fortunate survivor, Eichor (or Igor) Narodny, stood up, bowed low, and then sat him down again, smiling broadly, and bowing his head a little. The audience applauded him loud and clear.

The captain continued. "The remaining half-dozen groups, who elected to go look at things halfway around on the other side of the planet, have not been able to contact us due to the problem afflicting our electronic equipment. But we have their last co-ordinates, their longitude and latitude. With those data in hand, we shall go looking for them, starting tomorrow morning, some half-dozen or so aircraft.

"Sign up if you want to go with us on the search. I yield the rostrum to Dion for a few closing words." Dion then spoke briefly, reassuring everyone that all had turned out well despite the electronic glitches. Everyone arose, to return to their private chambers, or to one of the many bars aboard ship.

Dion, Verne, and Chris briefly retired to the nearby bar to consult briefly among themselves about ways and means for tomorrow's quest, the big search. They and their crew, or crews, would take several of the smaller spacecraft that could navigate in the heavy atmosphere that surrounded most of the planet apart from the polar areas. They planned to leave around 8 a. m., and to bivouac overnight either aboard ship or in whatever impromptu shelter that offered itself. Meanwhile the three alerted the night shift to make sure that the several spacecraft had plenty of fuel and provisions for several days just in case.

After several drinks the three retired to their private quarters, Chris and Verne in adjoining suites. Everyone would sleep well. They had gone through a demanding and very full day. No sleeping aids would prove needed, and the few drinks that they had consumed in the bar would only help them slumber all the more profoundly.

IX. The Big Search

"Great, here we are bright and early," Chris looked at Dion and Verne. "Let's see what this new day and big search will turn up!" They smiled and nodded at each other. They had almost finished breakfast at the head table in the big assembly hall or eatery.

Verne turned to Dion: "Let's alert the crews to be ready to take off in half an hour." Dion and Verne made their announcement one after another, Dion speaking primarily to instruct the hotel staff to look after the premises and the clientèle in their absence, and to keep things functioning inside and outside.

The spacecraft crews had already checked the several space vessels in which they would voyage, and had everything prepared to take off. The Big Three—as everyone had begun calling Dion, Verne, and Chris half-jocularly—went on board with their small amount of luggage. They soon checked everything out, and took over the command together, before the space vessels departed.

Once up in the air, the three continued to consult among themselves. Verne, once more Captain Laverne, observed to the other two: "We have a long trip ahead of us, halfway around RCP 100. But I think we can get to the general area late in the afternoon—the region where those half dozen crews elected to go, where they landed. We have the general directions, the general longitude and latitude. Wisely they chose a comfortable semitropical region a lot like that around the hotel-headquarters.

"Also, to make things easier for us as the rescue party, hardly any passengers insisted on going along with us unless they have skills in engineering and electronics. We don't yet know how much work we shall need to do, to get their electronics repaired and running again. Not to mention getting their aircraft up and away."

Under the direction of the Big Three the squadron of the spacecraft had made better time than anticipated. They reached the general area halfway around RCP 100—that was their destination—a little sooner than at first projected.

Captain Laverne to Dion and Chris: "Let us look using our most sensitive equipment for any signal at all that the ships of the half-dozen groups that came here might still be able to send out."

They were hovering above that general area, but whoever recorded back to the hotel that this semitropical region resembled that in and around the headquarters had erred. With a few clearings here and there the land lay well inland of any ocean, but they could see a few lakes and a big wide river running through the terrain.

Dion to Chris near the captain: "This forest might just as well be a tropical jungle, an impenetrable wilderness. Unless the expeditionary crews were able to land in some large glade, or series of glades, I don't see how we'll find them. Of course, we will locate them at some point, but it won't be easy. That is, unless we can pick up a signal from them somehow. The electrical storm from the sun must have hit them a lot harder than what it did in and around the hotel. We'll have our work cut out for us."

Verne and Chris nodded in agreement. Their squadron began reconnoitering the jungle beneath them in ever widening circles. But they found nothing, and received no signal. Just before sunset they landed in a very large glade near a big lake. Everyone would go to sleep early, once they had eaten. The beer and wine consumed with their meal helped them all fall into slumber.

The captain had improvised at once an all-night guard system or schedule in easy two-hour shifts to last through the period of sleep. Some of the crew would rest 8 p. m. to 4 p. m. but most of them would do so 10 p. m. to 6 p. m. A great silence descended over all the newly arrived spacecraft. Everyone seemed to sleep soundly. The night passed calmly, without incident, and with no rain or wind.

In conjunction with the captains of the other spacecraft, the Big Three, but above all Captain Laverne as the overall commanding officer for the entire squadron, had wisely decided that everyone should sleep aboard the space vessels rather than bivouac out in the open in this wilderness, just in case something seriously untoward might come to pass from hostile animal, gigantic insect, or anything else.

Meanwhile outside and beyond the squadron diverse forms of life padded or slithered with care and caution in the ever darkling jungle, all the darker as the space crews had noticed because of the absence of the moon or other natural satellite. Even with guards nobody outside would have slept well or soundly, no bivouacking out under the stars, almost invisible at any rate under the forest canopy.

At not quite 8 a. m., when the rescue expedition had not quite begun to move up and out, a knock on the main cabin door sounded loud and forthrightly. The captain himself went to answer and open the door. There stood Captain Zack (born

Zachariah) Doefin, the commanding officer for the half-dozen expeditions that had chosen to go halfway around RCP 100. The two captains greeted each other warmly, and Verne brought Zack and the escort party with him at once on into the main chamber.

Zack: "We heard you hovering over our general area yesterday, but with our systems down, completely, we could not contact you. No way could you have found our encampment with our ships easily from the air. We had parked under the tree cover, not expecting our need to be rescued."

Verne to Zack: "Nor had we expected the need for rescue!"

Zack: "But we figured out where you had landed for the night. And we started out on foot to find you about an hour ago. Here we are!"

Verne: "Welcome! We'll fly on over to your encampment under the forest canopy, and take you and your escort back with us. We'll figure it all out, and get you and your electronics back up, and then we can all fly back to the hotel."

Zack: "It may take awhile for us to do that, maybe a few days." And so it did; in fact several days. Meanwhile the chief navigator contacted the hotel-headquarters, to let them know the situation. All was in order, and they would soon have the systems failure corrected, but that it might require up to a week or less. Dion reassured the people in charge on the *Roosevelt* that they at the rescue site would not forget to set up the protective feature, lest another electrical storm from the sun screw up everything all over again.

With all the engineers who had flown with the initial half-dozen expeditions to the spot, plus those who had accompanied the rescue squadron, it took somewhat less time to get the systems failure corrected than anticipated. Dion made sure to activate the protective feature on all the original space vessels that had arrived there. At long last both squadrons could leave, and return to the big hotel.

X. All's Well That Ends Well

Here, where the world is quiet;
Here, where all trouble seems
Dead winds' and spent waves' riot
In doubtful dreams of dreams
"The Garden of Proserpine," A. C. Swinburne.

Following the minor emergency of needing to rescue the half-dozen groups from halfway around the planet, things proceeded for the Grand Tour without glitch or serious problem. It was a great comfort to continue living in the hotel-headquarters. The Big Three dispatched the passengers to their various destinations per their own preferences, Dion acting as the chief director or dispatcher.

Everything proceeded in a smooth and regular manner. These successful missions turned out as adventure enough for most of the clientèle. The planet never ran out of amazing locales geographically. Most of the passenger-customers avoided the coldest polar zones, but not necessarily the highest mountains often as cold as the polar areas.

One late. afternoon, just by chance Dion, Chris, and Verne found themselves off shift, and had changed into regular civilian clothes. They had agreed to meet in one of the bars (also an eatery) near the great eating or assembly hall. They sat at the end of a large oval table on the other side of the room from the counter at the bar. They were all nursing a large and "life-sustaining" cocktail, as Chris called it.

Dion addressed Verne and Chris in a pleasant and relaxed way. "So, what do you think now of this Earth-like planet? Does it still surprise you in terms of its variety and size? Do you still enjoy the duties on a space cruiser, or rather off ship here in the hotel?"

Verne: "As far as duties go, they seem a bit lighter than on a giant spacecraft out in space."

Chris nodded in agreement, and then he spoke. "Yes, this is an amazing planet, truly like Earth (but without the primates like us), and twice the size. Duty here as on our giant spaceship is in one sense more involved. We must often deal with passengers in a way we don't need to do on an enormous transfer ship collecting refuse and garbage from all kind of other (inhabited) planets, and then depositing the whole mess on a transfer world used only as a dump. Trash of all types has remained a problem for us primates since Greek and Roman times. As for the passengers Verne has to deal with them much more than I do."

He looked at Verne, who smiled before he spoke in turn. "The passengers are generally pleasant to handle, but sometimes one particular passenger can come up, and give me a hard time. However, my social-sensitivity classes have given me plenty of tools to defuse the passenger and the situation. I for one am still, and very much, enjoying this one world."

At this point some customers with drinks in their hands alighted at the other end of the big oval table. Verne spoke in a louder voice, and signalled to the party of middle-aged women and men, some six or eight of them. "Dear fellow passengers, why don't you join us here at our end of the table?"

The group conferred among themselves, and getting up with

their drinks they ambled over, sitting down next to the Big Three. Dion smiled, and said, "Welcome to our little party!" Of course, the new group knew who the Big Three were. The mood seemed open and friendly.

Dion: "We hope that you people are enjoying your Robinson Crusoe Tour on RCP 100?!" The newcomers responded at once. A handsome gentlemen spoke up, "Speaking for myself, and for the others in our group, I can give you a great big yes!" The others murmured their assent, offering appreciative comments: "Great! Fantastic! Astonishing!"

Next a beautiful woman from among them spoke in a carefully modulated voice. "Overall I too am enjoying myself as much as my friends here, and I have only one complaint, if complaint it is. But more a regret."

Dion looked up: "Please do say!" Encouraged by Dion's warm tone, she continued. "My friends and I are all experienced travellers, and have travelled in many parts of our Mother Earth. We enjoy old exotic lands (yes, they still exist), and old structures in particular, but here you have no ruins. We expected that, but it still is something that we miss, however illogically." She looked around at her friends, and then back to Dion.

"No ruins?!"

Dion: "What you speak is true in general, but we do have some ruins, although not as an ordinary destination."

The middle-aged clientèle at once focussed on Dion, who continued. "The first attempt to establish a hotel here like the Hotel Roosevelt, here where we are all staying, turned into a failure.

A pretty expensive one. The place was abandoned, once the

Outer Space Consortium had the present hotel built."

He paused as if arranging his thoughts and what he wanted to state. The passengers gave him their full attention. "I had not thought of it that way before, but you know the place does rather make for some impressive ruins. Would all of you like to go there for a day trip? It is not a dangerous locale. We can arrange it."

The half-dozen or so passengers conferred among themselves again, quickly reaching an accord. The beautiful woman with the carefully modulated voice answered: "Speaking for all of us, we would like that very much!"

Along with Captain Laverne and chief navigator Chris Owens, Dion had arranged a trip to the old original but abandoned Hotel Madison in its location relatively close to the Hotel Roosevelt, at least at no considerable distance. The Big Three had chosen what resulted in a beautiful day. The ruins as a good-sized group of interconnected structures rose up not far from the ocean but still in the semitropical zone, the climate warm but not unbearably hot. They all embarked in a single aircraft, and accompanied by another as a back-up in case of any trouble. The management did not wish in any way to inconvenience such high-paying customers.

They landed at mid-morning, and as Dion announced they would return to their usual hotel around midafternoon. Rather than a boxed lunch, the group had brought with them several chefs with their staff and plenty of supplies, drink and food. These added workers would make a meal outdoors so that everyone could eat comfortably alfresco. The trees would provide shade.

Meanwhile a service crew had gone ahead at dawn to check the location out. They made sure that it was in fact perfectly safe, and to cut away any growth that might impede the passageways from outside the ruins or into the interior, as well as all around it. The service crew had finished their task, and had left, just before the visitors arrived. They had also set up the ambiance outside the main entrance for the chefs and their staff to make the lunch. In addition they had set up the tables and chairs for the passengers and the Big Three in the ample shade. That way they could all eat in comfort without peril from beast or big insect. All was ready.

The two aircraft of the visiting party touched down, and everyone had disembarked. As an added precaution a few guards had come with them with weapons at the ready. The first sight of the ruins, the abandoned hotel, proved overwhelming. Rather than some Art Deco birthday-cake kind of construction, the architects had built it around a series of courtyards with one very large one in the middle approached from the entrance vestibule directly.

Although no more than six or seven levels high, many if not most of the flat roofs cantilevered or somehow projected outward, creating a somewhat fantastic appearance. Small bridges connected many of the roofs at different heights, contributing all the more to the fantastic aspect.

The visitors began discovering and exploring, and the Big Three accompanied them as intrigued as the passengers by the novel site and its varying perspectives. The beautiful woman with the carefully modulated voice came up to Dion, introducing herself again as Lady Guinevere Lenoir as she had done the night before. She repeated the same admonition, "Please call me Guin."

"Dear Dion, I forgot to ask you last night a perfectly obvious question. Why did the authorities abandon this ambiance? The location seems ideal, and the buildings themselves are most impressive."

Dion responded at once. "I don't quite understand the reason, the reasons. The official statement is this. That if a really powerful tropical storm were to strike, the site might prove untenable. The hotel stands not far inland from the ocean, as everyone can see for themselves, and not much higher than sea level. If an error to have sited the hotel here, then it was a strategic error. There is something else involved, but the powers that be have forbidden any further enquiry, and that prohibition extends to everyone, visitors or staff. That's the best that I can explain it."

Lady Lenoir smiled, nodded her head gratefully and graciously, and merely said, "Thank you very much!"

Chris to Verne: "What do you think?" Verne: "Quite a place! Even if abandoned, and buried here and there with vines and vegetation. Chris: "Dion's explanation doesn't quite answer why they abandoned it. But that's all the authorities allowed him to say."

The two had climbed up to the topmost level, and were facing the solid front door of a small suite. It was locked. Verne: "Let's go ask Dion for the set of master keys to this hotel that he's carrying. I want to enter these forbidden chambers." Some little time later they returned with the keys.

After trying out several, they unlocked the door, and entered. They found the original furniture in situ, and covered with dust, but not bad. Someone apparently looked after the place. The air seemed fresh, although warm, doubtless due to some clever ventilation system that did not involve mechanical air control.

Chris: "What a neat little apartment! Main room with kitchen and cabinets, bedroom, bathroom, and big closet. Even the books are in place." He picked up one by itself on the top shelf as if purposely left there. He opened it and found that it was a diary. On the title page it read "To whom it may concern." He handed it to Verne, who looked it over. He conned the neatly penned handwriting, and then read aloud the opening entry.

"Now that the new hotel has opened, the powers that be are letting me stay here as an unofficial caretaker. Yes, unpaid. I volunteered, but the new hotel will send over to this old one both my drink and food. I have plenty of water on tap. Let's see how long I last here at the Madison before moving over to the Roosevelt."

Verne: "Let's claim and keep this. I'll put it in your backpack. We can read it back at the new hotel. Let's join the others. As they left, they locked the door, and returned the keys to Dion. The latter smiled, but asked no questions.

The visitors passed the morning inspecting the old hotel's interior, as much as the vines and vegetation allowed. At noon thanks to the chefs and their staff, they had their outdoor meal outside the main entrance. After due repose the visitors passed the early afternoon inspecting all around the entire ensemble of structures. At 3 p. m. or so the visitors, the chefs and their staff, all flew back to the new hotel in the two aircraft. Everyone felt that they had experienced a fine and satisfying visit.

Once they had all entered back into the lobby, the Lady Lenoir came up to Dion to give him her thanks. "Thank you for a fascinating visit. Our little group has had a most enjoyable time of it. We hope that we might return there again, and soon. That old hotel does constitute some real ruins, quite impressive. The outdoor lunch turned out very well, indeed. Our compliments to the chefs and their staff. We shall see you three tonight at dinner."

RCP 100 seemed never to run out of unusual geography, above all on a planet double the size of Earth. Tremendous forests of deciduous and evergreen trees in the temperate zones. Challenging, overgrown, and overwhelming jungles in the almost unbearably calescent tropics, in particular where the equator circumferenced the globe. Utterly arid and lethal deserts in any zone, polar, temperate, semitropical, but preëminently in the tropical regions at the equator. The mountains in almost any zone that would have easily matched the Himalayas. Canyons so vast that they would have even dwarfed the Grand Canyon in northwest Arizona in the United States.

The different expeditions even revisited certain areas that intrigued and fascinated everyone who went there. Thus it was at the urgent request of the Lady Lenoir that her particular party of friends and/or partners returned to the ruins of the Madison Hotel, attended by the Big Three and the requisite chefs with their staffs and servers. They bivouacked inside the hotel, rather than outdoors, even if they had used some of the newfangled tents. They remained at "the Ruins" for several days and nights.

Whether there or elsewhere, luckily no glitches or misfortunes occurred. Even when they did—all minor, of course—the passengers merely thought them purposeful, as arranged by the Big

Three to give an edge of excitement or adventure to their expeditions. The Big Three enjoyed all this as much as the clientèle.

Meanwhile in their quarters when off shift, Verne had noticed a subtle but marked change in his partner's mood or behavior. One night the captain asked Chris, "Dear friend, something is bothering you. I noted it off and on while we stayed at our official Ruins! If I speak the truth, and something is eating you, please let me know. I'm all ears."

Chris assumed a serious expression, and then he smiled before speaking, "Since you ask, yes there is. Let me speak frankly, okay?" Verne nodded back.

"When we sought, and signed on for, a space cruiser, like the old-time ocean cruisers of the 1900's (gosh, how long ago that now seems!), I had thought that it would turn out a piece of pie, a piece of cake. I thought that I would feel as content as a cat confronted with a saucer of cream! Well, thinking about an agreeable possibility is not quite the same as actually doing or living it. The old problem of hypothesis versus reality. When we have completed the tour of duty on this space cruiser, I would just as soon return to a transfer ship. Of course, you will do what you think is best for yourself, whether or not you return with me to our old garbage scows."

Verne: "I was wondering if you weren't having some second thoughts. Thanks for letting me know! I've been having a few myself. Duty on a transfer ship is much easier for me. Here I seem to be at everyone's beck and call whether passengers or crew.

"I checked with Nate at Alphabet, and he tells me that the Outer Space Consortium are making all transfer and other voyages much shorter unless to a very distant galaxy. In fact a regular transfer run will now take only about two years or so. I could handle that if you could. Let's think about it. In the meantime let's go down to our favorite bar next to the big assembly hall, okay?"

Chris, with enthusiasm: "Yes, definitely! Thanks for the palaver. It *has* helped me."

Amid all the comings and goings, the expeditions and excursions, the outings and innings, Chris and Verne kept busy. Verne as the commander in chief of the *Enterprise* out on the water, not far from the Hotel Roosevelt, or in charge of the overall enterprise, qua enterprise, on the ground or in the air or in space. Chris as the navigator on anyone of the numerous aircraft or smaller spacecraft navigating allover RCP 100, on the land or in the atmosphere.

They continued their discussion about the possibility of returning to a transfer ship. Chris in fact had made up his mind; he wanted to go back to their old job. Chris: "I've decided at last. It's a garbage scow in space for me. There I feel most comfortable doing my usual job." Verne: "Well, I've decided the same. It would be much easier for me than on a big space cruiser, even if the amenities appear, or are actually, better in certain aspects. Let's do it then when we get back to Earth." The two smiled and nodded at each other in agreement.

XI. Another Big Decision

The residence on RCP 100 had reached its logical conclusion. The clientèle pronounced themselves quite satisfied with all the expeditions on the planet. The Big Three expressed their satisfaction in turn back at the passengers and their contentment.

Dion to Chris and Verne: "You, your crew, your staff, and your passengers, and what we've all achieved together, have all turned out great. Once you're gone, then we here will need to adjust to a much smaller number of people around us, and we shall miss all of you."

Chris and Verne, individually, each in his own turn: "It's turned out to be one fantastic experience for us all. But who knows? Maybe we'll all see each other again at some future time."

Verne: "Now let's see if we can lift the U. S. S. S. *Enterprise* up and out of the water, off the planet, and back to dear old Mother Earth!" It turned out much easier than anticipated, and soon the great space cruiser was speeding on its way back to their native planet.

Much time had now gone by. Once more aboard a transfer ship, their new one, Verne and Chris, once more off shift, stood before the large rectangular window that dominated the main chamber in the captain's own suite. On this new space voyage Chris and Verne had come aboard a much better and newer space vessel.

Verne: "You know, I never tire of looking at the astral panorama embodied by our own galaxy or by the nocturnal heavens at large."

Chris: "I feel the same. It always amazes and stuns me. It always makes me feel both humble and humbled. But that does not bother me! To feel that I'm part of this everything! It's exhilarating! That's enough to satisfy me and my little brain and my little ego!"

Verne: "Dear friend, you have stated my own emotion succinctly. Thank you!" Here the two faced each other directly, embraced, kissed, held onto each other briefly, and then disengaged, smiling as always.

Sleep; and if life was bitter to thee, pardon,
 If sweet, give thanks; thou hast no more to live;
 And to give thanks is good, and to forgive.
  "Ave Atque Vale," A. C. Swinburne (to Baudelaire).

Codicil Canticle Doctrine

The Lich of And/Or we cannot escape,
Nor yet the Witch of Endor as his mate,
Wherever we might pass in cosmic-scape:
Whatever might have happened as of late,
A petty destiny, or petty fate,
Wherever passable, with gap or gape:
Might render all amiss, amass, amate,
By subtle means of fish or fowl or ape,
And what is more, by cosmic jest or jibe or jape:

The older or more basic thought, monarchical,
 Is once again a something else—amiss, amass, amate—
Remains as ever, or however, hierarchical.

Art is not, cannot always be, but democratic;
And when the product of one mind, is autocratic.

ASTRAL DEBRIS

Poems in Verse and Prose

Contents

ASTRAL DEBRIS

Poems in Verse and Prose

The Toucan from Guinness

(On seeing the new Guinness logo c. 2019–2020.)

The toucan sits atop the weathervane,
The glass of Guinness sits atop his beak,
A potent drink when mixed-in with champagne;
A cocktail not unknown, nor else antique,
Whose impact one by one comes not oblique:
Hung over from Black Velvet's overdose,
When pain can change the proud into the meek,
And one awakes alert, not comatose;
The pacifist can morph directly from the bellicose.

So, let us not disparage such, the quiet and the calm,
That often can attend the daily alcoholic dose,
The sometimes artful drink, about which we need have no qualm.

Let us commend the glass of Guinness on the toucan's beak,
A something that we can acclaim, a noble drink unique.

Cult after Cult

Alas, the cult of God the patriarch
Has not been superseded by the true
Or basic one, that of the matriarch:
By whom you are not me, I am not you,
As we by chance are born, as if on cue
Without the mother none of us are here:
We are but phantoms in an endless queue,
As one by one we come forth to appear—
And yet how last the birth-bed may transmute into the bier!

Still, death and birth may come to pass in any place whatever,
Whether we walk across the moor, or plunge into the mere—
The cosmos rarely stipulates or dogmatizes "Never!"

This utmost awe, the pure sublime, can happen anywhere,
And we can view them as presented: naked, nude, or bare.

A Choice of Politics over Humanity

"And have we ever had before
a like mean-spirited régime
in Washington, D. C., as under Trump?!"
A question from a fellow poet,
29 February 2020.

True, this is one old tale, but such a tale,
One that goes back to Rome, or Babylon—
The need to choose between a home or food.
Why such a struggle over food and rent?—
Food stamps for some can mean to eat, *or not,*
While funds for food must go to pay the rent.
Is this political, or humanist?—
What of the single-parent families?
How shall those mothers and their kids survive?—and yet with grace?

And why should anyone have need to make this choice?
Could not society better apportion things?—
So that no one should be without food or a home?

There seems to be no choice, one must be rich or poor,
Or at best middle-class between the two extremes.

Ixaxar

I

"Ixaxar, or Ishakshar." Word and concept derive from the "Novel of the Black Seal," by Arthur Machen-Jones, 1895.

The black seal, a round black stone, two inches across. Engraved with some kind of cuneiform characters, like those in the Hebrew alphabet, a Semitic language. (Data for concept taken from the same source above.)

Ixaxar, pronounced not ik-zak-zar but ish-ak-shar, three syllables: Hermetic, Hamitic, Semitic. Hermetic as in Hermes, or Mercury, Greek or Latin, respectively.

The background upon which Machen draws (although not referenced purposely) includes Greek and Egyptian antecedents, Hermes, Mercury, and Thoth. Machen certainly ranks as an Hermetic and/or hermetic author if anyone does!

Hermes is the Greek god of commerce, cunning, eloquence, invention, travel, and theft. He serves, as the son of Zeus and Maia, as herald and messenger for the other gods in their grandiose abode or palace on Mount Olympus. Giver of increase to herds, guardian of roads and boundaries and trade. (Herm: a square stone column topped by a bust or head of Hermes, and used as a terminus to mark a boundary.)

Also, god of science, of luck and treasure-trove, conductor of the dead to Hades. His attributes include the wingèd sandals (talaria), wingèd hat (petasos), and the symbolic staff of a herald, the caduceus (two snakes entwined along the staff with two wings at the top). Mercury, almost identical with Hermes, and also identified with Thoth.

Ixaxar

II

Thoth, *Thoyth* (Greek forms of name), Tehuti (Egyptian), scribe of the gods, who measures time, and has invented numbers. Hence, presiding deity of wisdom and magic, the god of scribes. Correlate Egypt with Mesopotamia.

Babylon: c. 2225 B. C. the richest and most magnificent metropolis in the world, not barring Egypt or China. The Chaldeans became as famous for their magick (including astrology) as the Egyptians. Evidently considerable exchange occurred between the mages and astrologers of Egypt and Mesopotamia, the latter including Babylonia and Assyria, and later such outlanders as the Medes and Persians.

(Further data on Hermes.) Hermes Trismegistus; Hermes Thrice-Greatest. Is this Hermes as author-poet in human form? Legendary (perhaps historical) author of works embodying magical, astrological, and alchemical (alchemistical) lore, that is, doctrines. Could there have lived such an author in late Hellenistic (pre-Roman) or early Roman Alexandria on the Nile in the delta (with its bizarre mixture of Greek and Egyptian culture and architecture)?

Ixaxar

III

It was a black, unlustrous piece of rock
Flat, circular, an inch or more across—
Such as no shop would ever have in stock.
Not beautiful as a peacock with its gloss
Nor swan upon the lake, the stream, the floss
The black stone hid a glamour as from Tyre.
Perhaps it had been thrown into a fosse
But recently, as in a fit of ire,
That it did not turn out a gem replete with astral fire.

A rare seal found not far from ancient Babylon,
Lost or abandoned in the midst of muck and mire,
Someone perceived the stone's indented hexagon.

A thaumaturgic talisman, it could maintain its own,
The Hexacontalithos, or the awesome Sixtystone.

Hermes, Mercury, or Thoth

Whichever—Hermes, Mercury, or Thoth—
When we invoke their name, their immanence,
We do not hesitate, we are not loathe.
We call to them in all their eminence,
No less than in their full pre-eminence,
To help our cause, to heed our plea, our prayer.
We do not call them but at our expense—
Invoke them, but sincerely, and with care
They are more cunning than the supplicant: beware!

Who is this "we" that we so often cite as well?
Is it our better selves, an unknown excellence?
Or poet and his audience in parallel?

Beware of trifling with plenipotentiary gods—
Do not stand up against them, or the odds: those are the odds.

For Derrick Hussey, Literary Entrepreneur

To you, the Mage of Hippocampus Press,
As yet another chief of dream and rime,
You qualify as not one whit the less.
Through you so many other voices chime,
Rising above offense, misdeed, or crime,
Where fantasy can reign a little while.
Extant above the grimness, moil, and grime,
Free for a little from the common mile,
You make us glad to wander anywhere in any style.

That is a great good gift, both deft and debonair,
It guarantees the refuge of a castled pile,
Or some oasis of felicitous and fair.

Where one can tilt at horror, terror, panic, doom, and fear;
There you possess a paradise daemonic, dark, and dear.

The Hidden Ones Among Us

It was an Arthur Machen kind of woods
Where one might glimpse a vagrant nymph or faun
Emerging from their leafy neighborhoods.
These figures from an older faith have gone?
Somewhere beyond the sunset and the dawn?—
On into some fair never-never land?
But still a buck, a doe, with kid or fawn,
Do not seem startling miracle less grand,
And somehow safe past our et cetera with ampersand.

The old religions yet live on, it would seem everywhere,
By secret or clandestine means, by needed underhand,
So that the old autochthonous can pop up anywhere!

The vagrant nymphs and satyrs live among us human folk,
Disguised as us, the same as us, but always under cloak.

CODICIL

The old arts with their gods live ever on in fame,
In modus quite alike, if not indeed the same.
The old gods did not die, have never died
Somehow, somewhere, they manage to abide.

Correspondence

The painter is heroic in the everyday—
In workroom, in workshop, in studio—
The poet's mind serves as his atelier.

With easel, palette, canvas, oil, acrylic,
With brush, or palette knife, elsewise dactylic,
The unknown makes its more than essence known.

It makes its inscape or quintessence known,
With dab and stroke and line, with tint or hue—
And thus this is the modus of the painter-paladin:

Whereas the poet's images appear to come and go
Within the tight world of that cage—the skull, the brain, the mind—
In ceaseless flush and flux, in endless thrill or throb or throe.

Let us not underestimate a struggle quite unseen,
It is a sacred interlude, a limbo in between.

The Case of the Light Fantastic Toe

(Some random thoughts and lines concerning *The Big Toe*.)

What is important then about "The Life of Dance"?
It is the strongest symbol for "The Dance of Life,"
An intensification of the everyday.

So, why devote a magnum opus to the toe,
To the big toe, or to "the light fantastic toe"?
Because ballet remains the greatest art of dance.

We borrow some thinking at this point from elsewhere,
We take some thoughts from Havelock Ellis as his heir,
As they somehow concern the everyday, the commonplace:

Because among so many theses, as laid out,
Not all their master authors are as deep as he,
This aptly metaphysical psychologist:

About the virtuous aesthetics of our very selves,
Our physical reality, our physicality,
To be displayed upon a pedestal in public place!

"The Harp That Once Through Tara's Halls"

(Tara Hill, the seat of ancient Irish kings.)

The harp, the harps, that once for Erin's king,
Her own High King, made song on Tara's Hill,
Made metal strings through Tara's halls to sing.

So that the listening ears might have their fill
Of sadness or of gladness or of ill,
The lively strings would make a feast of sound.

Of Erin's vital green, her chlorophyll,
How many songs rebound, redound, resound,
That had their firstling source upon that hill, that ancient mound.

By means of random heart, from ear, from lip, from tongue,
Those melodies can still enchant or yet astound
When haply broadcast by the bellows of a lung.

We still can hear those older tunes upon the breeze
Whose beauty can yet thrill and make our heartstrings freeze.

Some Master Realists and Chief Illusionists

(On contemplating the trinity of artist-illustrators
Howard Pyle, N. C. Wyeth, and Maxfield Parrish.)

As soon as I learned to read in grammar school, I began borrowing books from the Juvenile Room of the downtown (or central) New Bedford Public Library, a solid shrine dedicated to reading and learning, the outer walls build out of granite. With the two tall (two-story) Doric pillars in front, with a broad and solid flight of stairs going up, the main library rather resembled a temple from Graeco-Roman antiquity.

Sometime before my tenth birthday and my mid-adolescence, I read and experienced the adventures purveyed in a series of good-sized hardcover books, mostly works of fiction. Childhood classics, one could call them, but both adults and children read them then, and still read them. Age is no barrier.

They dealt with historical, legendary, mythical, or just fictional subjects, such as Robin Hood, King Arthur, and so forth. But what made them stand out as movies that the reader could unfurl in his own imagination, they contained marvelous illustrations, reproduced from oil paintings in full color. Much later I realized some truly fine artists had created these pictures.

I cite their names in tribute to them, Howard Pyle, N. C. Wyeth, and Maxfield Parrish, although Parrish mostly did magazine covers, prints, and posters. I wish to thank these three. They made my latter childhood a period of enchantment.

Realism or Fantasy or Both

Howard Pyle, N. C. Wyeth (and whyeth not?),
Along with Maxfield Parrish, claim our praise,
And rightly thus, as well they should, or ought.
Whether of Sherwood Forest's autumn blaze,
Or of King Arthur's woodland chrysoprase,
With pen or brush our trio proved expert,
They placed their characters beneath our gaze,
Whether with plate or leather armor girt,
And sought to keep or save their flesh from harm or hurt.

When what else could divert, or could cause to desist,
Than sword or shield best for defense, thus to avert
Death or destruction, but the bow and arrow did assist:

Whenas the English archers made the French knights melt away,
At Azincourt, or Agincourt, then at that certain fray.

(N. B. The victory of Henry V of Angleterre
over the French under Charles VI on 25 October 1415.)

Das Kapital

Karl Marx (1818–1893) and Friedrich Engels (1820–1895).
A Tertium Quid or Quiddity: Socialism versus Capitalism.
"They must be some old vaudeville team—
                          I hear tell that their act is: capital!"

We choose poetics over politics—
Mishmash confusing, contradictory—
The latter worse than lice, or body ticks.

Marx and Engels, what formed their history
Is known, and now remains no mystery,
A team like London's own Magog and Gog.

Their lectures, staged, led to their victory,
Disguised as dialectic dialogue,
A tertium quid that has not parallel or analogue.

Ah, those two socialistic animals or angels—
With wit, with righteousness, with genius all agog
How they changed people's take on things, did Marx and Engels!

At this late date their message seems more needed now than ever;
Allow the infinite to play its part, and never to say never!

Justice for the True Cape Cod Folk

A word of praise for Mary Oliver,
Who sings in turn the praises of the Cape;
She stays the Cape's devoted follower.
A fan of Outer Cape, and Lower Cape,
As well of Middle Cape, and Upper Cape,
Her praise includes the little forms of life.
As friend of life in every style and shape,
She counters politics, their nonstop strife;
With which *our* politics seem oftentimes too rife.

She needs her hours of quietude, to make us her report,
To make her point as keen as that of rapier or knife,
As if convoked to show herself in some poetic court.

Outstanding fan of wonderland, of her own nature-scape,
Thus Mary Oliver protests the Cape's unending rape.

And on Towards Cocaigne

(Gâteau de cocaïne.)

N. B. *Pais de cocaigne,* land of cake.

Where might exist this country of Cockaigne,
That wonderland of luxury and ease,
A place where one would have no strife or pain?
A place where one would need to pay no fees,
A place without a need for locks or keys—
With other goods that would make paradise.
A halcyonic land with no disease—
A place beyond expense, reward, or price—
Is there a gate that might unclose by luck, by roll of dice?

There is no easeful gate or other access to that place;
There is no magic word to speak, or once, or twice, or thrice;
Entrance denied, we veer volte-face, on past disgrace or grace.

Alas, we shall not ever taste that special kind of cake;
All other baked goods will taste false, no matter what they bake.

Twenty–Twenty

The year of Twenty-Twenty, does it not
Yet also serve for human sight as gauge,
As measure from infinity to naught?
Thus Twenty-Twenty forms the page
On which to write of sage and chronomage,
And thus of vision in a deeper sense:
Of prophecy hymned in an earlier age
By errant prophetess in terms intense
With eloquence; nay more, grandiloquence; yet more,
    magniloquence:

The prophetess would sing of death, and of re-birth,
Of great good times, and then in utter contrasense,
Of ire and strife, of desolation and of dearth:

Let scholars opt the Twenty-Twenty to their taste,
The year, the vision, or the spectacle embraced.

The Promise of Infinitude

"The stars might urge, but they do not compel,
                      and they do not coerce."
          Quotation from an astrologer friend long since deceased.

The choir of stars—the suns and moons—stand guard
Throughout the vast and clockwork universe,
And over our own Earth keep watch and ward.
Agreeable conceit that we rehearse,
The night sky might confound, but not accurse,
Because without it none of us are here.
The cosmos is our mother and our nurse,
Confers the gift of limitless frontier,
To go beyond the boundaries imposed by love or fear.

Might we have erred to postulate this endless world as friend?
To reach and state this thought must we consult with priest or seer?
And it is not despair, but hope, that sees it without end.

By every right and wealth of wonderment *we* may conclude,
The Ocean Sea of stars makes real the promise of infinitude.

Renaissance

(The vernal or vertumnal season, 2020.)

What metamorphoses the seasons bring—
The wanton miscellaneous of green—
The buds, the blossoms, and the leaves of Spring!
Chrysolite, olive green, or olivine—
Chrysoprase, apple green, or viridine—
What treasuries of color, tint, and hue!
Blue grass, green grass, and grass aquamarine,
What viridescence burns before our view,
A riot and a rush that no one could refuse or rue!

After the Winter's dour, unending, barren spell—
What joyance this parade, procession, and review—
Without this renaissance our life would turn to hell!

Better than all the dreariness, the cold, the mordancy;
It saves our common life, this burgeoning of verdancy.

An Humble Tribute To a Friend

(For Paul Scannell, Thursday, 30 April 2020.)

A word of praise for Paul, our own Saint Paul,
Upon his special day, the thirtieth—
If no such word, then we have missed our call.
Then we have missed the right use of our breath,
To praise a great friend's life, but not his death,
Upon whose help we utmostly depend.
For him we do this on the thirtieth—
A gallant cavalier, a prudent friend,
Whose wise advice guides us, in our own turn, to bow and bend.

In sum, you have fulfilled three quarters of one hundred years
Across the seas of time and space, a world that has no end—
In sum, you have enriched this vale of laughter and of tears.

Some praise, please, for a teacher, a scholar, and a gentleman,
From one who signs himself in turn his humble partisan.

The Spirit of the Rose

Soulève ta paupière close
Qu'effleure un songe virginal;
Je suis le spectre d'une rose
Que tu portais hier au bal.
    "Le Spectre de la rose," Théophile Gautier.

"Open your eyes against the light
 Where dreams a maiden's garden-close;
I am the spirit of a rose
That at the ball you wore last night."

It was an elf-like lad garbed as a rose
In rose-red petals, but a sprite with force
To haunt your dreams with leap and pause and pose.
So, wherefrom had he come in all due course?
Had he escaped somehow from purse or bourse?
A cache of ghosts kept in captivity?
How had he left behind his native source,
To live in lightness or in levity,
If not forever, then at least in context of longevity?!

Cape Cod's Uniqueness

by Paul Scannell

Having a sense of North, South, East & West is
USELESS

Knowing Right and Left is
CONFUSING

Cape Cod is geographically a mixed up place
Yet, some of us get to where we want to be

Those folks divinely chosen to be born here
know everything

Wash-a-shores rejoice being able actually to navigate
and arrive on time

Wash-ups long for the conveniences of noisy and crowded
urban and suburban life

Our love of Cape Cod life is Unique
As indeed we are

Created 8 May 2020,
Friday afternoon

An Endless Coast

(Eastern U.S.A.)

The East Coast! from low-lying Florida
Out to Cape Hatteras, or Cape Cod sand,
Is varied all the way to Canada!
And beyond that, on past to Newfoundland,
Past Labrador, past one unending strand
Of harsh, unyielding rock, or gentle shore,
Made up of plain or rainbow-colored sand,
Reflecting then some kind of unknown ore,
Kaleidoscope of color, as from pale to that of gore.

A broad encyclopaedia of flotsam or of jetsam,
How much of it will sink, how much will end up on the shore,
Or in the gut of some poor fish, which will have drunk or et some!

Let us proclaim, to make the message fair and dutiful,
The sea and shore, although used as a dump, stay beautiful.

Sugarcane and Sugar-Coat

Somewhere between the winter and the spring—
Sporadic interlude of warm with cool—
How far their wild notes do the songbirds fling!—
Or do not fling at all. Am I a fool
I cannot hear their song?—am I ghoul
Or ghost that feeds upon some ghost remains,
Or is it yet again that echoes rule?
Or can I only proffer sugarcanes?—
The candy or the plant, and only echoes and refrains?

Better to give a sugarcane than give a sugar-coat,
Which when that vanishes, it also takes away all gains
As it reveals the bitter core, the truth beneath the bloat.

Better a model in reverse: the alligator pear:
A coarse outside but with a suave inside, a better pair!

Contrary Motion

Already Spring, I think about the Autumn,
And thus I go from the top of the year
Only by circumstance down to the bottom!
So I descend from the threadbare or the sere,
From optimism, down to dread and fear,
A transit that does not help reassure
My minuscule reserve of great good cheer,
But hope ensures the lure and then allure
Of best or better things, of wilding things and pure.

But time and tide demand that we remain alert—
If we forget, we must redeem by forfeiture—
For only when we sleep, might we repose inert.

In but one year do we travail from the height to the bottom—
From Winter to the Spring, from Summer to the Autumn.

The Doré Vase in Golden Gate Park

(Not far from the DeYoung Museum, San Francisco.)

More vivid than the news in some news-eum,
A sculpture that we would much rather face
Than all the sculptures held in the museum!
What sheer delight, this giant urn or vase
Made real by one Gustave Doré, a case
Unique unto itself, and from afar!
It moves in time at its own stately pace,
Congruent with the sun, the moon, the star,
And yet it never moves at all, a stance we could not bar!

Here we find *La Vendange,* in English as *The Vintage,*
Wine bubbling from the top, with bugs as on a jar,
A big tall urn, and metal-cast, as from a mintage.

Bless the person who brought it over, out from France,
To have as neighbors our own insects, our own ants.

N.B. Now inside the museum.

Enquiry

(For Dean Franklin Coffman II in friendship and esteem
on going around the sun seventy times.)

How many times have all of us not been recycled,
And in between our other lives in Otherwhere,
As well as on the Other Side no less recycled?
When in so many forms and shapes, and unaware
Of them as we might be—but why then should we care,
Except past lives or not, they all accumulate:
They all pile up to make us choose which way to fare,
To forge ahead before we might think it too late,
As if in answer to some prompting that might seem like fate?

Because you have become the dean of sonneteers,
In the selfsame way as one Adam Bolivar
Remains, and has become, the dean of balladeers:

No matter that your work might seem like caviar
Unto the hoi polloi, such is the way things are!

No matter!

Something So Small

Somewhere amid the woodland and the glade,
A tiny flower like an orchid bares,
However small, but brave and unafraid!
However it might happen, or it fares,
That something stomps upon it, unawares,
The flower is crushed, is gone, by accident!
So, who is there who sees, who knows, who cares,
To realize this lethal incident,
Or to lament its death, a life so small and innocent?

Metaphysical or Less

(An esoterical aside: that thirty equals ten times three.)

Our bodies are composed of particles,
Relentlessly by Time used and re-used:
Are we no more than things or articles?
By metaphysics taught or else bemused,
And by the mystical somewhat confused,
As we go guided by our animus—
Or by the heart transfixed, transformed, transfused,
Reason and health remain a total plus—
The cosmos, or the universe, is more than worth the fuss!

Howevermuch by our own senses oftentimes abused,
We stay much more than cosmic-astronomic detritus,
Howevermuch relentlessly by Time used and re-used!

The holy men, or yet gurus, are they but ghosts or ghouls,
And like philosophers, no more than wisdom's dupes or fools?

Astral Debris

("That could come fairly soon, although there is
no set date yet.")

Are we no more, or nothing less, than this?—
Than star dust, cosmic fragments, or debris?—
Before it falls on in the void abyss?
Stuff pulverized from massive down to wee,
Whether from elephant or honeybee,
Demands no end to metamorphosis.
But it demands an end to woe, or dree,
To take us back to mini-morphosis,
Awaiting some appropriate Eurydice and Orpheus.

The happy ending is convention or conceit—
A sweet *concetto* that might yet enhance or free us?—
While in a common dungeon where we all can meet.

Just constellated detritus is status quo enough,
As matter pulverized, reduced to nothing more than stuff.

Whatevery, Whatnevery

There is but calm and beauty in this place,
For contemplation and for reverie,
For each and every one we must make space.
For each and every one, for every,
Whatevery might come, whatevery,
Such seems to make the cosmic law.
The cosmos, it appears, whatnevery,
Permits not more than wonder, or but awe—
Is this advantage, disadvantage, or is this a flaw?

Despite our efforts to forbid, forfend, prevent—
The questions yet remain about the cosmic law—
Always we ask: What was intended, what was meant?

Our nervous primate energy always gives us no peace,
We cannot say to us ourselves: No! stop! leave off! let cease!

A Bit of Whimsy à la Leah Bodine Drake

A noble alexandrine for your thought—
Your image or your fancy or your dream—
For what it is, not for what it is not:
For your own gloss, your glamour, and your gleam,
Where your own fantasies abound, or teem,
As rich and ripe as any line of thought:
As any guide or specimen or scheme,
That might come to disaster or to naught,
For any point of view discussed, opposed, or fought:

We must unladen at some harbor or some port;
With cargo of "rare thoughts delight" too full or fraught,
Our ship is not a floating fortress or a fort.

She must find for herself a proper marketplace,
To find some commerce with both graciousness and grace.

N. B. "rare thought's delight"
    — Edmund Spenser, *The Faerie Queene,*
    Book VI, Proem, stanza 1, line 6.

Inarticulate

A simple Spenser stanza will avail
To lift our spirits from the uninspired,
As it so often does, and without fail.
Without the need to grasp what has transpired,
When passion makes us tense, or much too wired,
A lightning bolt can clear the mind at once.
It clears the mental cobwebs long acquired
Doubtlessly we would need to be a dunce,
Not to grasp this impasse, reduced to sighs or moans or grunts.

An Awkward Choice

Which represents the greater gain,
Does Averonne or Amithaine?
Does Amithaine or Averonne,
As limned or sketched against the dawn?
With finial or tower or spire,
Which looms the larger or the higher?

Whose ornaments are more grotesque,
What windows are more picturesque,
Whose Gothickness provides more light?
With detail more adorned or dight,
Can we perceive a maid inside,
Or yet an owl or swan outside?

Whose verdant gardens grow more lush,
Whose fountains do the sweeter gush,
To which belongs the rarer blooms
Amid the gravestones or the tombs?
An awkward choice at worst or best,
But worthy of a greater quest.

Some Writing Found on an Alley Wall

A sequence found on a wall in an alley,
Of white hand-written numbers all in chalk,
Why such a series, as this curious tally?
Thirty-one, thirty-two, thirty-three,
Thirty-four, thirty-five, thirty-six,
Thirty-seven. And it did not rime!
But next to it a pictured tomahawk,
As warning or as threat. But for what crime?
Why then this writing, as from some unpeopled pantomime?

And/Or

An existential balance and/or contrast.

The things of which I never tire, or would,
But first the trivia to push away,
And even with the will I never could!
Our Mother Nature, or our Earth today,
And with the things we wish might go away,
As we have signalized long-since before:
The things with which we must live every day,
Like our bacteria, the open door
To death, the passage to elsewhere, the promise of "and/or"—

There is no help or facile remedy for this,
Save death, or yet another place or life, and/or
Why would we wish to wander in the void abyss?

Impossible or possible, the and, the ought, the naught:
Whatever the varieties, there is no end of thought.

THE LADY LASS
WHO MAKES HER
GARDENS GROW

(For Gail Fryer Scannell)

Our Lady of the Gardens

(Notre Dame aux jardins.)

We do not hanker after orchids when
We have such irises more glorious
Than any orchids either now or then:
The upper petals, as pure impetus,
Make up a little cup as fabulous
As any demitasse filled up with mead:
Or some liqueur yet more mellifluous
Which fires the blood like riding on a steed
That finds among the asphodels a more than worthwhile feed:

The lower petals measure more than half a foot across,
Light blue or royal Tyrian that could not fire our greed—
This treasure is not gems or gold, or what might seem like dross:

If Beauty cannot feed the gut, and only heart and soul,
These irises might help negate, and if not quite the whole,
Then at least part of this our life's unending rigmarole.

The Lady Lass Who Makes Her Gardens Grow

We note the portents in the clouds,
The prophecies upon the wind,
The omens or the auguries,
As though from Cathay or from Ind:
The Ind is India, or Hindustan—
And Cathay is Cataya or Khitai.
                    Old Rime.

Once long agone, it seems, in a kingdom by the sea,
That into a democracy had somehow changed,
A democratical republic, or res publica,
Where Liberté, Fraternité, Egalité,
Or Liberty, Fraternity, Equality,
Had become the motto, the moral, or the ethic,
And everything was politically correct,
And all was well, and everyone was well besides:—

Yes, once upon a time in that locality,
Thus far away a lady lived with a few friends,
Out in the countryside, within her little house,
Surrounded on all sides by gardens manifold,
And people called her thus, Our Lady of the Gardens,
Ymchauntress was her name, and widespread was her fame,
A botanist and horticulturist of some renown,
Who had created new divisions of plant life,
Of fruits and flowers and vegetables, as well as trees.

When people came from near and far to ask for help,
Her counsel and advice on everything of plants;
She would hold forth in state from her old rocking chair,
With genial smile, with suave and cultivated voice.
She seemed at times a lady fair, high-born and reared,
But she claimed, as her descendance of simple folk,
Only from fishing and from farming families,
And that remained a status and a status quo enough.

For in her youth she had travailed across the globe
By jungle, by desert, and even pole to pole,
To find and study all the plants that she was able,
From polar, tropic, semitropic, and from other zones,
And she brought back the seeds, no less the specimens,
That she had gathered sparingly upon her route,
Or mailed ahead of her return much in advance,
She did not want that burden as she went from clime to clime.

Some seeds did well in her North California home,
Even if it was extant in a mild winter zone,
And these were tropic plants that proved hardier than thought.
She even grew some orchids in her little greenhouse
At once adjacent to her simple little home;
Within that special place she grew from specimens
Gigantic orchids and with strangeling goblin faces:
These epiphytes had come from the Amazon's own basin.

She even entertained some lovers on her way,
The better ones she did invite to visit her at home,
And who knows what might not have come of that, whenever?
She took her chances where she found them, as she could,
A practical approach, but somehow still romantic.
It left much open to the circumstances of the moment,
To happen, to develop, to elaborate,
To living in the moment of the here and now.

She had gone early to her greenhouse on that morn,
She had slept well despite her zeal to foment growth,
She was a-fervor to be planting her new seeds,
To see what they might birth, what they might not bring forth!
With her bare hands she had picked up some dampened earth
From the pile on her table, to put it in a pot
Prior to planting it with some exotic seeds:
She crumpled the earth in her hands, she loved the feel!

How much had happened to and through this common earth,
To this rich black, to this rich brown, this basic soil,
Yet still uncommon even following a million years!
As she was at the end of her youthful travelling,
Years agone, she was as eager now to plant new seeds:
She also wanted to plant outdoors both seeds and plants.
(Such patience with devotion do gardeners not show?!)
Thus Ymchauntress would pass her days in botany.

As for companionship, she had her dogs and cats,
No more than several, but those more than sufficed;
Plus the occasional house-guest, staying overnight,
A single person, perhaps a couple, no more than two,
Who would sleep in the one other, or extra, bedroom,
Someone from the U. S., or more often from overseas:
She had as many fans as friends of every type,
But only botanists or horticulturists.

The only problem that remained was that of food,
So people brought their groceries, or pre-made meals,
For supper or for dinner or for break-the-fast,
But also beer and wine, or other alcohol—
Ymchauntress was no prude, or shameless teetotaller,
Even if on occasion, a coffee-or-tea-totallist.
Her only moderation was that one imposed
By horticulture or by botany or both.

So much for practical details and other necessaries;
The everyday, the commonplace is where we live:
And splendor or epiphany? They might inspire,
But also tend to burn us out, and leave us desolate.
We cannot live forevermore in ecstasy,
For exaltation, or exuberance, demands a price:
There is a fee for faerie gold at midnight;
Thus have the ministries of chance and law decreed.

THE LADY LASS WHO MAKES HER GARDENS GROW

Upon a clear and sunny day there came a lad,
And on sabbatical from his academy,
Who drove up to her house in modest rented car
Sometime around midmorn, and thoroughly prepared:
He brought with him both drink and food—and specimens
As fabulous as faerie gold at midnight or alchemy,
That problematic, and/or worse, forbidden art,
To change base metal into gold at great expense.

He had achieved, or re-achieved, a noble quest
And for the tulip, as the national Dutch flower.
This graduate student, a botanist, Hans van Trinker,
Had brought some bulbs for two varieties of tulip,
The black and purple-black: the concept of the black
Variety had long preoccupied, even obsessed the Dutch
For centuries, since the fifteen or the sixteen hundreds;
The purple-black was his own innovation, yes, his own.

Prepared by letter and by phone, the lady lass and Hans,
They got along just fine, and hit it off at once:
As horticulturists they thought almost the same!
They had a great exchange, and Hans had planned to leave
The tulip bulbs with her, to visit on the fly,
But she convinced him to stay on, for several weeks,
While they would grow these novel tulips from the bulbs,
And thus they came to flower, the black and purple-black.

One the younger, one the older, these handsome two,
They found themselves attracted to each other.
The meeting of their minds led to that of their bodies,
As indeed often happens in the course of things,
No big surprise, and Hans stayed on yet even longer.
They were both otherwise unmarried or unattached
For that moment, for the nonce, or thus it seemed,
But as always complications did exist.

Meanwhile their making love turned out spectacular,
And tender, nuanced, passionate, no less compassionate.
The passion for the two together burned the same,
A rare concordance of mind, body, heart, and soul.
She raised the subject of parenthood, that is, for them:
She had never wanted children, to be a mother.
Not an issue for Hans, he had fathered children in his youth,
And those two had remained for him more than enough.
Now young adults, they both were well, and doing well;
He did not need to fret for them at all.

"If you want me to stay, and continue our relationship,
  Then I must get a job as botany professor in some college here,
  And retire from the University of Utrecht."
  Hans had spoken, looking at Ymchauntress all this time;
"I can do all of this while on sabbatical."
  She spoke, "You may do what you want, as you prefer,
  But, yes! I would love to have you here by my side."

As graduate student and as teacher's aide, not yet
A bonafide professor, but still on sabbatical,
Hans had to wrap things up at his home in Utrecht.
He would perforce be gone awhile, several months,
Before he could return to Ym's embrace and life.

Meanwhile the Lady Ym could take on other students,
And in this case Olivia de Andrade,
A young lady from Brazil, to study horticulture,
And even from Manáus, the old-time rubber capital,
Whereat the Rio Negro meets up with the Amazon.

Olivia spoke perfect English as well as Portuguese:
Tiny, slender, olive skin, and more than pretty,
She was beautiful, with lovely mien and manners.
Ym took delight to have her as a live-in student,
And regaled her with the stories of her visit at Manáus:
Thus a special bond was forged between the two.
Olivia turned out to be exceptional
With much experience of things botanical.

What is more, she could cook, and had attended cooking school!
Her family was old money from the rubber boom,
And her parents escorted her to the Lady Ym's abode
All the way from Manáus, by plane, by train, by car:
Olivia would thus enrich the Lady Ym.

Yes, indeed, she would enrich the Lady Ym,
And in more than one way, as pupil, and as one who paid:
Her parents insisted on paying a little more
To guarantee their daughter's residence with Ym.
Of course, they spent much time, if not the most of it, outdoors—
On her own part the girl was thrilled to learn from Ym,
Who could not help but recall the greenery around Manáus,
Cumbrous, humid, exuberant, and intertwined.

Olivia regaled the Lady Ym with stories of her own:
The epic fights or rivalries like those once waged
By the Dutch for the rare and singular or single tulip:
The lethal fights within the basin of the Amazon,
The epic fights, and for the choicest epiphytes,
Among the jungle folk and/or among their Euro masters,
The latter quite unknown for kindness toward the aboriginals,
Both anywhere and everywhere, wherever they had gone.

As positive enactors on the cosmic scene,
Mesdemoiselles Olivia and Ym have saved
People and values otherwise extinct or lost,
They did so, simply by their tilling of the soil
For flowers, fruits, and vegetables, and thus by husbandry;
And their example did more good, in calm and quiet ways,
Than great pronouncements, than grandiose announcements,
Than empty promises made by politicos.

THE LADY LASS WHO MAKES HER GARDENS GROW

Hans telephoned from Holland, and from historied Utrecht;
Evening there, but morning in the north of California:
"Here things are taking longer to wrap up than I had thought.
But maybe in a month or so, I should be back."
The Lady Ym responded, "Come back when you can.
Meanwhile I have Olivia to keep me company,
And to instruct; and we are doing well together."
Hans and Ym confirmed their love for one another.

Meanwhile Olivia and Ym were working miracles
Inside the little greenhouse, in that protected space:
With the specimens brought from Brazil they had fomented
A whole display of a dozen giant orchids
That flaunted the richest of Tyrian red-purples,
So dazzling and so vivid that they took away the breath.
Even Olivia admitted that they had
Not quite looked. so splendiferous back in Manáus.

At long last Hans returned, and Ym and he were overjoyed
At this reunion, and he to meet Olivia.
He complimented Ym on gaining a new friend,
A kind of adopted daughter, even if Ym was no mother.
He also brought some tasteful gifts for both of them,
But his gift, the most welcome, turned out to be some bulbs
As chosen by a friend, a tulip specialist,
Who guaranteed his choice would please the horticulturists.

Like everyone else Hans confessed him amazed,
Astonished, and entranced by the orchids from Manáus:
Never had he seen anything quite like them!
But he promised them, that Olivia and Ym
Would be equally pleased by the tulips from Utrecht:
Not only unusual colors but something else,
Some novelties perhaps that they had never seen;
Here he smiled a sweet smile, mysterious and prim.

Thus it came to pass that Olivia and Ym
Did in fact plant the exotic bulbs from Utrecht,
And watch them sprout and grow, the novel tulips from afar:
First the leaves, then the stem or stalk, and last the blossoms.
And even if a Hollander both born and bred,
Hans became as fascinated as the horticulturists
When watching the whole pageantry unfold and unfurl:
The process was always the same, but yet not quite.

What ravishment to watch a blossom bud and bloom!
Life, all of life, is magick, is a miracle!
From bacteria to bathysphere to biosphere!
Meanwhile Hans got himself a job as professor,
A privileged position teaching horticulture
At Sacto. State College that later metamorphosed
Into California State University at Sacramento,
An easy commute from where Ym had her house.

The house of the Lady Ym did not stand on the floodplain,
But higher in the hills northwest of Sacramento.
Elsewise the novel tulips did show something new:
Novel, unusual tints and hues awkward to describe,
But almost like a rainbow in diversity.
The five petals of these lilies' cups, the very flowers,
Had alternating colors, or one color alternating with white:
This novelty excited both Olivia and the Lady Ym.

Hans even brought some of his horticultural classes
To see the novel flowers that Olivia and Ym were growing.
The tulips? They seemed grand, indeed, and maybe more than that,
But it was the whole display of giant orchids
That flaunted the richest of Tyrian red-purples,
Imported from the Amazon, that stole the show,
That pre-empted everybody's fascination
More or less—only a very few preferred the tulips.

Some of Hans's pupils became so fascinated
That they decided to become horticulturists themselves!
And/or as teachers like Mynhyr Hans and Lady Ym.
But both of them admonished the students thus besotted
To consider this choice of career deep and long and hard;
That to become horticulturists, it might take many years.
It would require a demanding preparation,
And so much more than an initial enthusiasm.

Olivia had taken some young man to one side,
And quite a handsome youth, whom she was entertaining:
A geography major, he wanted to learn about the Amazon;
They were discussing Manáus, where the Rio Negro ends;
Manáus, he noted, stood at the conjunction of the two rivers,
Some two hundred miles or so south of the Equator.
His parents had promised him for his graduation
The gift of travelling in Brazil for several months.

Perhaps, she suggested, that they could go there together;
He could at least visit her family in Manáus.
Meanwhile she decided that she would stay in California,
And set herself up as private horticulturist,
If Hans and Lady Ym would sponsor her as legal resident:
They readily agreed, and thus all was decided.
Olivia had also reached an agreement with the young man—
Their attraction proved mutual and instantaneous.

Codicil: Nothing more now needs to be recorded.

COSMIC CASTAWAYS

Further Poems in Verse and Prose

Contents

Cosmic Castaways

Further Poems in Verse and Prose

Or/And

The brief reversal of the phrase, And/Or—
More properly, conjunction, to connect—
Is not a simple prank or jest, a dor.
What would you say if we might not correct—
In fact that is in essence to confect—
The word and/or connective to Or/And?
Should we apologize with face abject
For our faux pas? How should we countermand
For something so much less than grandiose or grand?

How do we find an Emily Post of grammar etiquette?
And if we do, how do we manage to reverse command?
Highlighted by some fountain and its single super jet?

How often must we bring the matter up in mode regurgitive?
Either *Or/And* or *And/Or*? Thus always an addendum or alternative.

The Known Unknown

The known unknown? Most of the universe—
Remains inextinguishably immense,
Past comprehension, or a piece of verse:
Beyond computer modelling, and tense
With cosmic energy, beyond intense;
Only with mathematics might one grasp
The scheme of things, a gutless confidence,
Research and search, and at long last to clasp
A poisoned sapience, like the cobra or like the asp.

What is to do with wisdom that is disillusion,
A disenchantment that is better to ungrasp,
In order to regain the primary illusion?

Metaphysics might comfort further than philosophy—
    through fantasy or fancy—
Through magick, through the supernatural,
    through misnamed necromancy.

The Heart Remembers

"The heart remembers," when the mind forgets, or thus we hope;
  Reality might dictate otherwise, or thus we find.
  All our life we have heard off and on this one quip:
"It's only in your mind"—it is all in the mind;
  Without it and our speech, we simply don't exist.
  Reason and mind and memory form our essence and our core—
  Without instruction we are lost—we must learn everything:
  Growing up and education take a long, long time.
  There's nothing radical in this, in what we state,
  Only profound generic truth, and that is all.
  No revelation nor yet any revolution
  Need apply in this case, just a dose of common sense.
  Despite the agony of loss we must move on;
  As we age, we need recall but our best memories;
  As we all fade away from life, from this our world,
  May a few still remember us, with kindness and with gratitude.

The Heart Remembers

II

The heart remembers but the mind forgets?
Sometimes both mind and heart lose memory.
Half a century of loving partnership,
Including children and grandchildren,
Ever so slowly eroded from within,
While the one takes good care of the other,
But the other does not know, nor could not,
What is happening to body, mind, and heart:
Prolonged farewell, more than tragic, beyond mere words.
A friend can only express empathy, sympathy, sorrow, and love . . . .

The Little People

The Little People, of which Machen writes—
One Arthur Machen Jones—or rather hints,
Are not as Walter Disney might portray,
Diminutive, or picturesque, or cute:
But alien, hideous, hairy, squat, and strong.
They lair in places underground, remote,
Out of the way, and do not seek our kind:
An interview by them in covert woods
Is not something to wish, but something utmost to avoid.

On our chance walks in Gwent, in southeast Wales, on
    Machen's turf,
By great good luck we did not come upon these "little folk,"
Lest otherwise we could not now report that we had not.

And this chance meeting, or this interview one did not have,
Would have occurred, in centuried speech, some fifty years
    agone.

Elizabeth the Second: 2020

(Born 1926—regnant since 1952.)

Today we have just learned, from the Sunday issue of our local *Cape Cod Times* for 14 June 2020, that on 21 April of this year, Queen Elizabeth II turned ninety-four, yes, 94! Such longevity as person or as monarch takes place only under exceptional circumstances. She has remained a calm, decent, composed, collected, and sensible human being, no mean accomplishment for just a little less than one hundred years, passing through much tumult in the world external to her life and monarchy. All hail, and congratulations!

She still reigns, not only de jure but de facto, and remains a beloved icon in the hearts of her subjects, as well as in the hearts of many other peoples who share the common culture and language propagated out from the British Isles since at least about 1580 via Francis Drake and other audacious adventurers and navigators.

She thus remains the Empress of the British Empire or Commonality, as well as (metaphorically) of the English language wherever spoken or written or printed. BRAVISSIMO!

(Chorus: Cheers and hoorahs!)

Unending Parables

Whether as tiny particles, combined
Or recombined, or entities complete,
Celebrities, fit to be wined and dined:
But everything, too easy to delete,
Remains as is, belongs to an elite
Of humble odds and ends, a lexicon:
A Wikipedia as daring feat,
Encyclopaedion Britannicon,
That never ends, that cannot end, as endless lexicon:

Because as lexicons they rate as cosmic parallels,
Unending sets of volumes that go on and on and on,
Are such not in themselves enough of cosmic parables?!

No wonder Théophile Gautier, truly "le bon Théo,"
Loved lexicons, down to their final "ah," and their final "oh"!

Chess or Checkers, Which Came First?

I

In that dim time when there was no life quite like us,
Ourselves, unless a primate form from Outer Space,
Could they have brought with them some kind of checkers
    or of chess?
Checkers or chess, what is the choice for us to opt? Olden
    Enquiry.

Foundational definitions:—

Checkers, a game played by two persons on a checkerboard with thirty-six squares, arranged alternately by color (usually with twelve pieces), each player having twelve checkers apiece, and thus overall two sets, arranged in rows six and six, on opposite sides of the checkerboard.

Chess, a game played by two persons on a chessboard with sixty-four squares, arranged alternately by color (usually with sixteen pieces), each player having sixteen chess pieces apiece, and thus overall two sets, arranged in rows eight and eight, on opposite sides of the chessboard.

Chess or Checkers

II

And even if I cannot play the game of chess,
No less a game of purest judgement, wit and skill,
On those chess pieces I might selfsame often muse:
This game of chess and its traditional morceaux,
How sculptured, picturesque—an ancient heraldry:
Over thousands of years they reach us on through time,
Over thousands of miles they reach us on through space,
This game is much more than a game, it is philosophy and life
    together!

From left to right the chess morceaux are neatly ranged:
Castle, Knight, Bishop (High Priest), King, Queen, Bishop
    (High Priest), Knight, and Castle.
The row before them consists of eight pawns, the foot soldiers,
    the pieces of least power or value, but useful (sometimes es-
    sential) for all the other pieces as first listed or registered
    above.
Chess thus derives from India, Ynd, or Hindustan, passing
    across the countries of the Middle East all the way to the
    Mediterranean, to Africa, and to Europe.

Puzzlement

Sometimes there is a space between events, not long,
And that is when, unplanned, we might accomplish much,
Enough to pen a poem, a dance, or yet a song.
Despite demurs Art is not ever a mere crutch,
Whenas it has us in its hold, within its clutch,
For Art is often consolation—on its own—
And in that realm of Art might we not stage a putsch?
Despite the critics—let them bitch, complain, and moan—
And if they cannot quite condemn, at least they might condone.

Like foreigners from Outer Space, outlanders from the Void—
For Art is often elsewise linked, is rarely on its own—
Like interlopers from the O. E. D., or from the "O. E. D."

Might there not be nirvana for our lexicons,
As something past our heptagons, or hexagons?

Disjunctive Autobiographica

Once more and clandestinely he had gone to the Zoo located in that park south of the old city centre in Sacramento, the state capital of dearest memory, in summertime, a season and a place of genuine warmth, if not of tropical heat. Not for him the hyperboreal delights of Arctic or Antarctic latitudes!

This zoological garden as ever gave him a vital shock, as from electricity, a reminder that, so far, our human stewardship has almost wiped out not just the mammalian and other native species, but even our insectoid brethren whose presence helps us all to grow, to eat, to prosper.

To help us all to do all that in an alien period that we inadvertently produced, not thinking ahead of consequences. Attention, pay attention, to these long-due bills delivered for payment, these emergencies that we might have avoided, if we had paid attention in advance. Where are the Cassandras to save us, all of us, from our fate?

Let us give leave for us to say farewell to these kingdoms of existence condemned to die by means of our own carelessness.

Exotical Preserve

How much time had passed since she, Elena Spartakos, as a teenager—but now a middle-aged and experienced gardener—had visited a glassed-in, old-fashioned conservatory, a greenhouse like the one that she had first visited as an adolescent!

What a treasure-house of temperate warmth in the coldest winter, a treasury of exotic plants the seeds and specimens of which had come together here from the zones all over our planet, the torrid, the temperate, and the frigid!

The floral examples alone took away her breath, and renewed once more the initial thrill or shock that first visiting a greenhouse in winter had given her. At fifty years of age she felt inspired again almost as powerfully as when she was passing through the earliest part of her adolescence.

What a rush of inspiration and aesthetic expansion! She nearly fell down, and had to hold on to a corner of an old wooden table near the main entrance. What a revivifying and viridescent odor, more than a fragrance, a drug-like incense! She soon regained control of herself so as not to disturb the several other visitors in her group.

How much this hothouse preserve of plants and flowers kept flourishing so very much from far and near!

Exotical in Perpetuity

The lady Elena had lingered behind in the greenhouse while her group went ahead to adjacent parts of the gardens that formed so large a portion of this estate, centered (of course) in the magnificent mansion, in truth an enormous palace, built long agone at the fin-de-siècle around 1900.

"I'll catch up with you in a little bit," she had called after them. "I want to spend a few minutes more with these unusual plants." They understood her passion and her need for a longer time in the greenhouse, even if she did not actually linger that much longer.

Once again—how many times had this not happened?!—Elena was impressed by how pervasive, if not ubiquitous, the different hues of purple and lavender extended all over the planet, whether among the common or uncommon flowers. Here she found the small, clipped-like blossoms of the Siberian iris that survived in that uncharitable place and climate. The lavender bouquets of lilacs grown indoors, and restricted to shrubs kept as little as possible. Gigantic irises of Tyrian purple, no less than gigantean tropical orchids of purple-black. Elena sighed. What a surfeit of extravagant beauty! Reluctantly she left the greenhouse to catch up with her companions.

Exotical Epiphany and Apotheosis

As Elena walked over to where her group of gardener-friends were standing in the shade of some unknown blossoming trees (although not native, they prospered here it seems perfectly well), a thought struck her almost like a light cardiac stroke or a shiver of lightning, a thought that she had contemplated on many occasions earlier in her life.

She knew that the remote rodent-like ancestors of the primates, including human beings, did not appear on the scene in the far-off Age of the Dinosaurs until—except—at the same time as the very first flowers. Thus in a sense the cosmos fomented humans and flowers at the same time, almost as if the cosmos prospered humans in order that some living entities could appreciate the wanton beauty of the world with depth and nuance.

Dilemma

Alas, the irises have gone
With all their flaming loveliness,
Quite vanished, disappeared, withdrawn:
Into what realm, and might we guess,
The true locale that more or less
Demands, commands, our pure attention?
Not so today, we must confess,
Too much distracts us from intention,
From our imagination and from our invention:

The very richness of the affluence today
Distracts us from our sole, from our unique intention.
How could it not, from what we purpose us to say?

The price we pay for what we speak—is that too high a price?—
To speak out, or only in terms of decorous, neat, and nice?

SOVIET SCIENTIST MORPHS INTO REFUGEE

A Modern Narrative in Verse

It was only a little article in the local newspaper,
It was only a little article on some back page
Of the business section in the local newspaper,
In the *Cape Cod Gazette*—the modest headline ran,
"Soviet Engineer Requests American Asylum."
The article, it read in part as a local item:
"Ivan Ivanovich Skiyevsky [the last name
Is given elsewhere as Skeeyefsky or Skiyevski]
Has requested protection from the U. S. government.

"He is a well-known construction engineer in Leningrad,
Who specializes in big dams, outdoor and indoor arenas,
But has achieved a few constructions classical in style,
Which harmonize well with the older Petrine buildings.
He was also a high-ranking member of the Communist Party.
Mr. Skiyevsky seeks asylum in the U. S.—
He fears for his life should he return to his native land,
And all because of politics he disavows.

"Denounced by one close friend for his critique of Soviet Russia,
Skiyevsky was warned by another but closer friend
Not to return to his home. The local powers that be
Let him depart in peace. He has bank accounts elsewhere,
In Western Europe (France and Britain). He is unmarried,
And has no or little family back in Russia.
Skiyevsky speaks flawless English and other tongues;
At six he began to learn languages in school.

"His case is now before the Committee on Foreign Affairs.
He does not seek financial aid, only refugee status,
And has already received several job offers."
So, what then should he do? So, with his tourist visa
He decided to travel throughout the U. S.,
Beginning with the West Coast. He flew to San Francisco,
Where he had distant relatives long settled there,
And prominent in business and in politics.

Although Ivan did not have any great faith or belief
In the Holy Writ of the Communist Manifesto,
Which had near put him in unholy bodily danger,
He was curious about the U. S. Capitalistic system,
As to how it really worked, that is, from day to day,
Whether or not he was prepared to swear his fealty.
Meanwhile he much enjoyed his forays into U. S. literature,
His true adventures on into the pure unknown.

While in San Francisco his distant relatives became
True family and true friends: poetry they all preferred,
Whether in Russian or in U. S. or in British English.
Especially they did advise him to pursue,
Knowing his taste for Poe and for romantic poetry,
That he should get to know the California Romantics,
A special group: George Sterling, with Clark Ashton Smith,
And Nora May French, but not to leave out Jack London.

Above all Ivan adored Pushkin and other Russian poets,
And even if these Californians did not resemble him,
They had a quality, and of their own, closely related.
Their cosmic-astronomical approach attracted him,
Perhaps like Tyutchev, but different and exotic.
This Ashton Smith, who struck great fear to Ivan's heart,
He spoke in terms like Holy Writ, or like Miltonic,
And yet they did resolve at last in existential mode.

Meanwhile Ivan did fall in love with San Francisco,
As one of her most recent lovers and *conversos!*
Who could resist that City by the Golden Gate?
One day he read upon a plaque on Russian Hill,
"To seek and find in little things the utmost quest,
That is the real adventure, but unknown to many folk."
So, no great undertaking need apply at great expense,
The real safari passed inside, shared but with friends.

Ivan? He much enjoyed the Russian tongue bespoke
With his own distant relatives long since in residence.
They introduced him soon, and to a woman his own age:
They fell in love at once, and married each for the first time.
Ivan would not return now to Sankt-Peterburg.
He took a job with an East Bay construction firm,
And at a goodly salary—they took care of the paper work,
No less his citizenship: it all received approval.

No more, no mere, asylum status for Ivan!
Meanwhile they had agreed: no kids. Their relatives
Had much more than enough to go around for everyone.
They might "adopt" a niece or nephew for their favor,
No more than several, thus perhaps just a few,
That would assist the children's parents quite a bit,
But which to choose, among the kids, the greatest cause:
They could among themselves rotate the kids ad libitum.

Ivanka and Ivan had chosen for their church
A Russian Orthodox with golden onion domes
Where they would wed, out in the Outer Avenues,
Not distant from the sacrosanct Presidio,
Nestled amid its luscious greenery adjacent to the ocean.
Although Ivan lived now far from Sankt-Peterburg,
He could not have felt more at home than where he was,
Where no compatriot could have betrayed his trust.

Meanwhile Ivan pursued his other quest, his other dream,
How did Capitalism measure up against the Socialistic?
Both had their faults and virtues, but Capitalism
Permitted greater freedom to the individual,
Rewarded much more that individual's initiative,
More than a state-run enterprise, thus from the top down:
Ivan reached this political conclusion on his own,
But it did help him to discuss it with Ivanka.

She, born and bred, thus in the north of California,
But mostly in Eureka, and in San Francisco,
Had studied Soviet Socialism on her own,
And had in her own way attained the same conclusion:
Capitalism worked out better, by far, than Socialism,
And for the greater mass of people overall.
He hated to reduce all things to politics,
But sometimes one could not help from doing so.

How could we otherwise explain great poets in our midst,
Often unknown, no less unsung in their own turn,
Until sometimes posthumously, even if no solace to them.
At least Capitalism permitted them somehow to survive,
 It did not put them into jail for what they thought,
But just ignored them for the nonce, until re-found,
Republished, they went on to found new schools of poetry!
We cannot blame posterity for their ignorance.

Ivan felt luckier than most, and thusly did Ivanka,
To stand aside, to think and feel, but for themselves.
Ivan at last felt free without the specter at the feast,
Of someone always checking over him, over his shoulder,
With which he grew up in the Soviet Paradise.
Better by far to be ignored than sent into Siberia
Amid the cold and ice of uttermost indifference!
Meanwhile the other consolations do exist.

There is art, there is love, on past the desert of depression,
As Baudelaire reminds us all: Get drunk on wine;
On poetry, yes, poetry; on virtue, or on what is right;
But with no violence or malice toward anyone!
Yourself remove from bad vibrations and from evil;
Defend yourself when so you must, but otherwise move on.
Dear reader, pray forgive us as the moralist,
This homily, didactic, stupid, obvious.

Now once upon a time in a kingdom by the sea . . . .
(An aside: by right, by righteous, and by righteousness.)

N. B. Despite appearances, despite seeming to be a narrative in hexameter blank verse as in previous collections or in earlier sections of the present collection, a certain amount of the story is prose arranged to look like verse, and hence it is a pure experiment. Certain prosy details of everyday life do not fit easily into a metric pattern, or not at all. Although the overall piece lacks the somewhat stricter meter of our earlier narratives, it does vaguely follow the rhythm of the alexandrine, or the hexameter, the rhythm thus acting as some kind of guiding principle.

INFINITUDE AND THEN RETURN THEREFROM

Yet Further Poems in Verse and Prose

Contents

INFINITUDE AND THEN RETURN THEREFROM

Yet Further Poems in Verse and Prose

A Slob-ocrat

One thing I love about America,
That ethnic-wise it forms democracy,
It does not lie far off, like Serica:
It is here, much more than mobocracy,
The real thing, and no mere mock-ocracy,
Better than silks or satins from Cathay:
And if we make a true slob-ocracy,
Then I, too, am a slob, right now, today,
And I am proud to claim it, yes, in every way.

Yes, I am one with all those peoples who protest,
And that we always can do thus, like yesterday,
Remains the surest proof, the harsh and acid test.

In mine old age I find myself aligned with Walter Whitman,
I can but praise. I never could be hatchet or a hit man.

Nonsense or a Koan

I have perused Nat. Geo. Mag., since five,
Since I was five, reading the photos first,
To learn how much the world remains alive:
Not just the human race, sometimes accurst,
But more than often blessed, as if rehearsed,
As cosmic powers observe, and leave alone:
Let life learn life, while quite in life immersed,
With no escape from koan or from cone—
Let us repeat—a secret koan or a sacred cone.

A place as free and atmospheric as the sky,
Let us take refuge in that corner, quoin, or clone,
A chance oasis, caught in haste or on the fly.

I seek a place to sit around, to hang out, and to loaf,
And is the Q the key, the cue, or yet the koph or qoph?

All metaphor remains and/or as if:
And is that sacred cone a symbol-glyph
To sacred mountain, some Mount Everest?
There let the matter lie, there let the issue rest.

And Yet Another Eden

The gardeners had laid the garden out
Which blossoms would go in what blossom bed—
They knew their challenge as they walked about:
Which plants by fountain or by fountainhead,
Whose moisture would make good, or might make dead,
According to botanic protocol:
With subtle care the blossoms must be fed,
No less than vegetable, not folderol,
A challenge from pure circumstance, and from the weather's all:

To existential circumstance all farming stays at risk,
The fate of planting and of growth, per Nature's protocol,
As either too deliberate, or otherwise too brisk:

No happy medium except in some abstract domain,
Perhaps the Other Side, where each and every thing remain.

Carnival or Nothing

It was the music of some carousel,
So overwhelming that it broke my dream;
The darkest night remained, no carnival:
No, moon, no stars, where only shadows teem,
Where only empty nothingness might seem
Like evanescent figments in my mind:
The carousel had somehow lost both sound and gleam,
The darkness had left nothingness or naught behind,
Left but a sense of loss, a vacant frame of mind:

I did not feel depression, or *mélancholie,*
 Just absence of the sensual, but still a bind—
Without our senses, we do not exist, we cannot *be.*

Give us bright lights, loud sounds, harsh tastes, and vividness,
A life alive with passion or with lividness.

Thesis and Antithesis

My poet, I dream neither of beauty nor of evil.
—Clark Ashton Smith, "What Dreamest Thou, O Muse?"

For some to live in manner nonreligious,
To live without a credo or a creed,
Might seem. the summit of the sacrilegious:
Always duality in word or deed,
Is that our punishment, is that our meed,
For thinking in our mode, as we insist?
Wherever might we cease the urge to heed
Duality?—whatever could assist
Us to escape this thinking, in which we persist?

To live life without passion, rapture, or enthusiasm—
Unconscious entity, and/or nonentity (could such exist?)—
Would be as if to live within the Void Abyss, the Empty Chasm.

And where amid the wide vocabulary of our tools,
Is that supreme one that might stop us from acting like fools?!

Forgotten Statue

I

Pilgrim Kinderfolk, an unusual name. His mother had named him after his uncle, her brother but not brother-in-law. He had favored his only nephew as a special companion as the latter was growing up, not far from his parents' house. The nephew had virtually lived with the uncle until the latter died, and the nephew had just turned twenty-one. Meanwhile he became a gardener, a landscape specialist.

He began with his uncle's property, and the estates of the uncle's neighbors on all sides. The uncle's estate, three or four acres with a big house but not a mansion, occupied a mostly wooded, parklike region, on Cape Cod, in the Upper Cape south of Sandwich, a choice area. At his uncle's death, as his will had laid it out, Pilgrim inherited the estate. There he continued to live, to make it the center of his business. Like his uncle he had not married, nor did he intend to do so via a conventional union. But he soon acquired a male companion, also a gardener, one Rick (or Richard) Richardson. Combining their livelihoods, they became quite successful. They maintained and transformed estates throughout the Cape and Islands (Martha's Vineyard and Nantucket).

Meanwhile they had almost neglected their own property, and had entered into a legal partnership both personal and professional. They both took the month of June off to rehabilitate a distant grove of black Lombardy poplars overgrown with vines, if not in fact almost hidden under them.

Forgotten Statue

II

After surveying the grove—noting what needed to be done, and how they would proceed—'Grim and Rick got to work at once. Eschewing any other crew, one early morning they approached the entrance to the grove with machetes in hand, well-sharpened. They would work almost with their backs to each other with a careful space between. Systematically removing all the vines from the front to the back of the grove would require much labor, and then much cleaning up.

They had parked their heavy-duty work truck nearby. A few heavy-duty wheelbarrows stood near the entrance to the grove. They had also brought with them some sturdy metal ladders. They began to work in earnest about eight o'clock.

Using ladders and wheelbarrows they had cut all the vines away from the poplars at the entrance and somewhat inward, but not as much as they hoped. This was a task that they could not now underestimate. Whenever later that June they would have removed all or most of the vines, they would extirpate the bottom stems and extract the roots. That alone would represent a major task, and second only to the removal of the vines entangling all the poplars.

By midmonth 'Grim and Rick had cleared the vines, and had hauled the debris to an organic dump not far away. Then with special machinery they extirpated stems and roots, the equipment making the whole process much easier and faster.

Forgotten Statue

III

The twain had found at the end of the grove a kind of adytum, or sanctum, an innermost sanctuary. The grove with the pillars formed by the black poplars served as a kind of outer temple. They both frowned.

A sturdy gate confronted them, and barred their further progress, a door made out of hard tropical wood with two panels opening outward, and set inside an Egyptian-style door frame made out of local stone, but locked with a massive iron lock.

'Grim suddenly had an inspiration, and smiled. "Let's go back to the house. I think I know where I can find the key. My uncle may have mentioned it several times."

No sooner had they left than they returned. 'Grim had found the massive key inside his uncle's desk inside the library. He inserted the key inside the lock, and after some finagling he managed to unlock the gate. They went inside, and found to their amazement very little dust, and no vegetal growth.

There, solidly positioned upon a broad but low-lying altar like a plinth, they noted at once a life-sized statue of exquisite workmanship, apparently made out of limestone, and painted in part like the statues in antiquity. The simple roof had preserved the adytum's interior and the statue.

Forgotten Statue

IV

They rivetted their gaze upon the image. It was a young satyr about their size and age. He had small beginning horns emerging from his curly mop of hair. What held their fascinated gaze? The sculpture seemed to be Pan combined with Priapus, the special god of Lampsachus in Asia Minor.

The deity has seated himself with his legs crossed before him, and rising from his crotch there stood up in all its splendor an enormous phallus, almost up to his neck: beautifully shaped, flesh colored, and with the foreskin near completely rolled back, that is, downward.

'Grim and Rick looked at each other in mute consternation, but both were grinning. 'Grim now spoke. "I remember my uncle telling me that he had purchased some sculptures in southwest Asia Minor—today's Anatolia—at the ruined site of Aphrodisias, the town where they made the best sculptures in the Mediterranean basin. This must be the chief piece. This happened in the late 1930s when you could still do that. So here it is, back here at his home on the Cape."

Rick rejoined: "Well, whatever it is, and however it got here, your uncle was a true connoisseur. It is better, I'm sure, than anything like it in any museum."

Postscriptum and/or Codicil

Late June, the big house, the library. Rick and Pilgrim are sitting in the big leather armchairs facing each other in front of the fireplace, the latter without a fire, of course. Summer.

Rick: "The air conditioning is fantastic with all the heat and moisture outside. But let's continue our discussion. Do you think that people back in antiquity, in the Mediterranean, actually believed about their gods in a literal way?"

'Grim: "What do you think? You were raised like me as a Roman Catholic. How much did you believe in what they said?"

Rick: "As a kid I said nothing contrary to what they preached. But like you I had my doubts, quite apart from Jesus Christ, how he lived, what he said."

'Grim: "I had my doubts as a kid, even before I began reading about religion, and how it dogmatizes." He had paused, as if gathering his thoughts before he spoke again. "Remember, there was no overarching church in the ancient world. Everywhere a huge abundance and variety of belief, but in one sense deity existed everywhere. No Inquisition, no torture. You could believe whatever you wanted. In a sense back then religion was a real democracy."

Rick: "Yes, I now realize it again. The Church of Rome did not yet exist, to preach one belief, and to force everyone to believe it on pain of death and/or damnation."

The Country Mouse and the City Mouse

The country mouse and the city mouse were having a lively chat,
The country mouse was tall and thin, the city mouse short and fat.

Both properly arrayed in their own business clothes,
Somehow the two had met by sheer coincidence,
Thereat, the western or New Jersey end or side
Of the George Washington Bridge, that high and noble span.
This was a place where rodent business men hung out
To carry-on the commerce of their rodent-dom,
The hifalutin rats, the smaller modest mice,
But everyone appeared to get along, and business boomed.

The city mouse, both sleek and plump, with fancy suit,
Had evidently done quite well in real estate,
Quite well rewarded by his fancy clientèle.
The country mouse, a farmer, dressed in overalls,
Had survived, had done well, but rather modestly,
Had a decent bank account, and seemed content.
The two were arguing the merits of their own lifestyles,
Country living vis-à-vis the grand metropolis.

The question was: Which one was better, or was best,
But the answer depended on each one's experience.
They reached a compromise: each would visit the other for one
    week.
And then decide as to the merits on both sides,
The relative advantages and/or the disadvantages.

Country and City

First the city mouse came to visit the country mouse,
Where he lived in an old, still viable barn,
Not distant from the Ramapo Hills in north New Jersey.
The city mouse took the Rodent Underground there and back,
The best way to avoid those pesky human beings.
The country mouse dined and wined his guest as best he could,
With wholesome country fare, with his own house-made wine;
He took him to the local sights and other spots.

In spite of his best efforts, those of the country mouse,
The city mouse longed to return to his Manhattan home.
The country mouse went back with him on that return,
So that he could then spend his own week in the Big City;
Where—dined and wined in his own turn, and in high style—
He witnessed Broadway shows, and visited museums.
He found it more than dazzling, but he missed his rustic peace,
And said goodbye to his old friend and host, with thanks.

Before he left, the two discussed yet once again
The relative merits of the urban versus the country life.
The country mouse as always would prefer the countryside,
The city mouse as always would prefer Manhattan.
But each one did concede: that each might work out well
Per the individual: and on this point they reconciled.

INFINITUDE AND THEN RETURN THEREFROM

Arse, Arsis, Thesis

Arse, however else defined, is Ass;
It might involve an Arsis and a Thesis,
But with an "r" it might possess more class:
And in this context it is more than Thesis.
Much more than Thesis or Antithesis,
Or beast of burden, but intimacy:
And for our human kind, perhaps with foetus,
Not democratic, but autocracy—
Two lovers in their time make up an aristocracy:

But love, or sex, allows an open playing field,
Which makes in turn that which defines humanity;
We cannot prophesy what future times will yield:

And for this we give thanks, no less than halleluyah,
No less than your attention and your ballyhoo-yah!

With Arsis, Thesis, and Resolve

With downbeat, upbeat, rhythm, and resolve,
Along with sexual desire as goal,
A point around which all things else revolve:
The one thing that is not under control,
Whether in small part or yet in whole,
Is Eros the Erotical, and wild:
But sexual desire is more than rôle,
It is the dynamo from wild to mild,
In plants and animals however formed or styled:

In humans it can often verge close to insanity—
By its enchantment most of us remain charmed
    or beguiled—
It guarantees all future life and continuity:

But just as love, or sex, could humans do without,
Or any living thing? On this there is no doubt.

Morceau Number Fourteen

What? Have we made it past infinitude,
A number we might call infiniteen,
Much less an age than it is attitude?
What? Have we made it past number thirteen,
Into the refuge of number fourteen,
Which lines up with the sonnet's fourteen lines?
For this do we possess a special gene,
Whereby we might end with those number nines—
Does this not more than consummate the number of those lines?

This exercise in minor numerology,
We do not mean as text that in-between combines
The pleasures and the rigors of theology.

Well might we rest us now, thus after so much labor,
When we might greet each other as our dearest neighbor?

Farewell

Farewell to metrics, metronome, and meter—
This news need not disturb us, nor convulse
We measure still by gallon or by liter?
We spice our food with condiments like dulse,
A flavor we should welcome, not repulse,
As we wend on our gastronomic path?
By measured spoon or cup, by measured pulse,
It all adds up someways, you, do the math—
For this you need not be a genius or a polymath.

You can get by with patience and with observation,
By prudent application of that which one hath,
With frugal and with steady usage, and with conservation.

We have lost sight of our goodbye, of our farewell.,
That we spoke at the start, forgotten like a spell.

Another Dilemma

"That I nigh ravished with rare thoughts delight"
                    Edmund Spenser, *The Faerie Queene*,
                        Book VI, Proem, stanza 1, line 6.

How facile to begin with verse or prose
A poem, than to sustain or to conclude,
If other than a prayer, a pause, a pose!
It goes beyond some blessèd interlude,
One with "rare thoughts delight" the most endued,
A sanctuary and a place to rest:
As if with some rare wine more than imbrued,
Surpassing so much else more manifest,
And in the same way so much else in origin and interest.

Too many choices and/or possibilities—
The inescapable "that is" and/or "id est"—
More challenging than some impossibilities!

At times life is too rich, thus too much like the universe—
The cosmos always goes beyond one turn, one only verse.

Carousal, Carousel, Merry-Go-Round

Carousal, carousel, merry-go-round
Only the latter two, so named, equate
In junction and in style, cycling around:
Their wooden beasties, how they match and mate,
As they pop up and down without abate,
With strident music, that of carnival:
Such music might wake up those dead of late,
No need for ghosts, no more than minimal,
But all real revenants appear much more than maximal!

How often everything recycles round and round,
Ordained by fate, in circumstances optimal
If not ideal, whether in substance, style, or sound!

And is it seven, seventy, or seventeen,
That mystic multiple, that prime infiniteen?

Parnassus Revisited

(Leconte de Lisle, 1818–1894.)

That noble *examplaire* of Le Parnasse,
Have we forgotten dear Leconte de Lisle?—
A somewhat startling oversight, hélas!
His many perfect poems keep their appeal,
If image into solid might congeal,
Like elephants across a moonlit waste.
From modern surfeit how he makes us heal
Antinomies his subtle plan embraced
Through Baudelaire, and then Rimbaud—and boldly faced.

His noble alexandrine functioned like a ship,
And kept French poetry upon an even keel,
With novel forms and themes, with lofty craftsmanship.

Was it a subtle Madagascar influence, inspiring heart and lung,
That shaped his voice, imbibed from Malagasy folk,
   and from their voice, their tongue?

The Concept of Cape Cod and the Islands

Vacation land of sun and sand and surf—
Including its own National Seashore,
How zealously Cape Cod protects its turf!
No less the two big islands add yet more,
Including all their history and their lore,
They all add to the local affluence.
This wealth goes back beyond the merely hoar
To time pristine—its lasting influence—
The place and people are the total sum, the present sense.

That it should last beyond our time, it needs therefore
Enduring vigilance and care—it follows hence
That all of this necessitates yet even more.

Let all of us who here reside not fail this test,
Not to erase this text from history's palimpsest.

Elements of an Older Prosody

(Something this poet-author hath long desired to say.)

A little definition or discussion seems useful here at the start. Among the many books on poetry as art and craft, quite a few proffer logical and historical information. The earnest reader might consult them. By definition, the new or newer prosody involving free verse end free form, can turn out as almost anything in any way. Basically we owe Walt Whitman for instituting via his *Leaves of Grass* a liberated poetic technique or prosodic technology. His new method has allowed people to state what they want whereas the older prosody apparently does not. Still some poets use the elder method or methods. It helps them to form or formulate what they wish to say.

The older prosody derives from that or those of Greek and Roman poetry with much use of diverse metrical patterns. (Technically a wizard, Swinburne comes the closest to creating a similar effect in English.) From Greek and Latin the inherited prosody became adapted to the new Latin vernaculars, the Romance languages, including Italian, Spanish, French, and Portuguese among others, and also by the new Germanic languages including English (Anglo-Saxon with many Romance elements) and German. But some of these prosodic elements exist in the Scandinavian and Slavic languages as well, not to mention those of the Middle East and the Far East.

A curious paradox. People speak of a certain musical poetry, but poetry is not the same as lyrics or verses adapted to song.

Question: Which came first, dance or song? Probably both at one and the same time. The older prosody, what to state? What a rich confusion and mélange it appears, it remains! Stanzas, topics, terms, forms, etc. For example, sonnets are not the same as dance and song, but they do dance and sing in their own way. Per single but related languages the accents may shift from one language to the next, Romance or otherwise. And in the given language the accents can shift from noun to verb, from adjective to adverb, and so forth. The student learns all this changing accentuation word by word.

Whether as poet or as any writer, we all must use the lexicon. However, a lexicon can only handle basic facts and figures but cannot handle (of course) undeclared phenomena, those that have not happened yet, however they turn out, never mind anent poem, or poetic form, or song or dance, specifically.

We leave the patient reader with this undigested paragraph of linguistic elements! Strophe, antistrophe (à la catastrophe). Arsis, thesis. Octave and sestet (one sonnet form), no less than sextet. Thesis and antithesis. Monometer, tetrameter, pentameter, hexameter (ad nauseam). Stanza, quatrain, quintrain, sestina: what, no sextain or sextrain?

We remain grateful that, when we began as poet, we managed to find, create, recreate, and feature two new forms, that we have employed almost exclusively since then: the Spenserian stanza-sonnet and an expanded form of blank verse.

Spenser Stanza-Sonnet

Let us end with a Spenser stanza-sonnet,
That glamourous amalgam or mélange,
With stanza, tercet, couplet primed upon it:
Like grapes fresh from the vintage or *vendange*,
Or items laid out on a bed or lounge,
The form can yield much of its one and all:
With so much space or stuff, no need to scrounge,
And parsimony only can appall,
As when inside a Spenser tower-castle's one great hall.

Whenever the old-fashioned turns exotic with new power,
The minute nuances will thrill and, what is more, enthrall;
How quickly then the past becomes a refuge and a bower!

Thus Spenser's own interior décors always appear deluxe—
With only small acknowledgement of topical caprice or flukes.

www.ingramcontent.com/pod-product-compliance
Lightning Source LLC
Chambersburg PA
CBHW050401030726
47503CB00006B/1959